Praise for
A Perfect Day to D..
Stories

— A finalist for the 2019 Eyelands Book Awards, Greece —

A Perfect Day to Die reminds me of what I love best about the short story form. With elegant, deceptively simple prose, Yoko Morgenstern unravels ordinary immigrant lives, revealing glimmers of hope even within darkness.
— **Tanaz Bhathena**, author of *A Girl Like That*

These wary newcomers with their jagged stories won my heart. Yoko Morgenstern offers a glimpse of the Toronto you don't see.
— **Katherine Govier**, author of *The Ghost Brush* and founder of The Shoe Project

In these insightful and diverse stories, Yoko Morgenstern explores challenging subjects from how the horror of the atomic bomb still lingers through traumatic memories over seven decades later, to how a character has a revelation after recognizing subtle signs of an ill-fated relationship, to even unveiling a novel perspective on the age-old dilemma of whether to be or not to be.
— **Rob Jackson**, Managing Editor Emeritus, *Great Lakes Review*

Told with economy, acute sensitivity, and flashes of piercing wit, the stories in *A Perfect Day to Die* are indelible. Yoko Morgenstern's deftly drawn characters struggle with mid-life dissatisfactions, yearnings, and childhood secrets. Their searches for meaning and intimacy unfold in Toronto, Oakville, Ubud, Tokyo, and Nuremberg, each place evoked with tactile precision. The past continually haunts and subverts the present. Even when the characters reach the brink of despair, they find glints of redemption in humour and sensory pleasures. A snack of *taiyaki*, a memory of *Satsuma-age*, a bowl

of soup: all take on symbolic resonance. Propelled by an irrepressible appetite for life, these characters and their stories beguile and enthrall us.
— **Kateri Lanthier**, author of *Reporting from Night* and *Siren*

Yoko Morgenstern's sublime stories are inhabited by characters defined by their tenderness and yearning. As their narrator, she skillfully invites us to empathize with their longing for hope, comfort, and meaning.
— **Rui Umezawa**, author of *Strange Light Afar*

A PERFECT DAY TO DIE

STORIES

GUERNICA WORLD EDITIONS 50

YOKO MORGENSTERN

A PERFECT DAY TO DIE

STORIES

TORONTO—CHICAGO—BUFFALO—LANCASTER (U.K.)
2022

Guernica Editions Founder: Antonio D'Alfonso

Michael Mirolla, general editor
Peta-Gaye Nash, editor
Interior and cover design: Errol F. Richardson

Guernica Editions Inc.
287 Templemead Drive, Hamilton (ON), Canada L8W 2W4
2250 Military Road, Tonawanda, N.Y. 14150-6000 U.S.A.
www.guernicaeditions.com

Distributors:
Independent Publishers Group (IPG)
600 North Pulaski Road, Chicago IL 60624
University of Toronto Press Distribution (UTP)
5201 Dufferin Street, Toronto (ON), Canada M3H 5T8
Gazelle Book Services, White Cross Mills
High Town, Lancaster LA1 4XS U.K.

First edition.
Printed in Canada.

Legal Deposit—Third Quarter
Library of Congress Catalog Card Number: 2022934029
Library and Archives Canada Cataloguing in Publication
Title: A perfect day to die / Yoko Morgenstern.
Names: Morgenstern, Yoko, author.
Series: Guernica world editions ; 52.
Description: Series statement: Guernica world editions ; 52 | Short stories.
Identifiers: Canadiana (print) 20220184968 | Canadiana (ebook) 20220184992 | ISBN
9781771837132 (softcover) | ISBN 9781771837163 (EPUB)
Classification: LCC PS3613.O7455 P47 2022 | DDC 813/.6—dc23

Contents

For J

A Perfect Day to Die

Erika thinks it's a perfect day to die. It's sunny. No ribbons of cloud in the transparent blue sky. Who'd think she was depressed because of the weather? She hates the blue sky. So painful. It's like Zumba when you aren't feeling like a party. It's like the feigned Christmas spirit when you aren't feeling like a family reunion. Great that Pink Floyd sang blue sky and pain.

The February air is ice. She's at Lake Ontario, near St. Catharines, off the QEW. On the other side of the lake lies Toronto's skyline. The needle of the CN Tower. But to the left of it looms another skyline. Is it Mississauga? It looks bigger than Toronto.

She plods along the frozen muted shore. On the beach, cigarette butts, popcorn bags, condoms are scattered. Beer bottles poke out between the rocks. She walks on. A crushed Tim Horton's coffee cup rustles under her foot. And another Tim's.

This unbuttons an old memory. When her daughter was small, they joined a shoreline clean-up with daycare teachers in Oakville. C'mon, it's Oakville, thought Erika, standing on Navy Street, looking at the gazebo. What was the clean-up for in this perfect beauty? The lake flickered in the sun. Sunshine through the leaves dappled the asparagus-green lawn, crewcut. The red of the mini-Oakville-version of the Peggy's Cove lighthouse. Yet they ended up with several bagfuls of garbage, mostly from Tim Horton's. "This is a true Canadian experience," a Chinese mother said.

Erika is 43. A perfect age to die. She didn't want to kill herself at age 39 or 40 because people would think it was a midlife crisis. She doesn't want to wait till 44 either because, according to her Japanese background, four—*shi*—is phonetically the same as *death*, and so 44 could be *double death*. No. Forty-three is good. It doesn't mean anything.

The reason for her suicide ought to be a mystery. She doesn't want anyone to figure out why. A death wish was her childhood friend. But she wouldn't like the ripples of feelings her suicide might bring to people's minds.

Actually, she doesn't really want to commit suicide. More precisely, she wants to quit living. Quit existing. As if she wasn't there at all from the beginning. She wants to disappear, stealthily, the way no one noticed the Little Mermaid turn into bubbles.

Erika grew up in an old bungalow near Rebecca and Bronte in Oakville.

Her father was an alcoholic. If not one, then a person who drank excessive amounts of alcohol. She didn't know the difference. He might have been the latter because he kept a decent-paying job. He was almost never home. When he was, he ran his fingers between his daughter's legs.

That happened just a few times. Just a few. Fingers-between-the-legs. Or fondling in the bathroom. But that wasn't the worst part. The worst part was that he didn't remember anything the next day.

Her mother didn't seem to care. Erika had never seen her mother care about anything. Or think. *Your father*, her mother said, *had designed a perfect life for me*. He ordered her dresses, enrolled her in a culinary school. All she had to do was to follow the railway track that he'd laid for her.

That was the childhood of Erika the only child. Her childhood ended early if she had any. A childhood with a hell of a lot of time with adults. She wasn't allowed lessons like other girls. No metronome, no ballet tutu, no gymnastics leotard. During holidays her parents took her to high-end resorts where her father could play golf and get drunk. No Marineland, no Canada's Wonderland, no Great Wolf Lodge.

Erika was often left alone in the backyard. A time-out, which meant her parents didn't want her around. When she was seven, Erika coiled a twine around her neck and pulled both ends, gently, steadily, pulled and pulled. Thinking that her real mother was somewhere out there.

Growing up without a role model, perhaps she was naturally attracted to mature people. Men or women, it didn't matter. She married a 38-year-old man when she was 18 and moved to a small town in Northern Ontario. She wanted to go far, far away from home.

Soon her husband turned out to be a boy. Life in a small town ruined her soul. But she didn't know what to do. She didn't know what confidence was, though she knew she was smart. Her looks weren't catastrophic either.

One thing she noticed as she grew older was her anger toward her parents. She never knew it'd been there, but once she realized, it grew and grew. The anger made her neither a good mother nor a good wife, she feared.

She stayed until their daughter got into the University of Toronto; when she moved out, so did Erika. Now she didn't have to pretend anymore. She could enjoy herself, the misery-oriented person she'd grown to be. Every night she sipped a bottle of wine, weeping, watching random videos on YouTube that she called *sad-boosters*, such as the last scene of *Les Parapluies de Cherbourg*.

One day she got tired of weeping. It was spring; she'd only noticed when she saw pictures of cherry blossoms someone had posted on Facebook.

She started to seek the timing of her exit.

Her daughter had just started her MBA in the United States. Still a bit too young, thought Erika, but she'd be fine, for she'd already found the most reliable, life-long partner: her strong self. So, Erika thought it was okay to die. But there had been one issue: pain.

Like Dr. Schopenhauer had said, Erika wasn't afraid of death but of pain. She went online and looked up a suicide guide.

Each suicide method was 5-star rated.

Hanging: the king of suicide. Convenience: 5, probability: 5, pain: 1. You'd immediately pass away, feel almost nothing. Okay, sounds good. The downside is possible fecal incontinence, or eyeball protrusion. Oh yeah, she'd heard about that. Not very nice for the stranger who found her.

Self-defenestration: if you land right on your head, you'd feel no pain. Erika imagined herself being on the top of a high rise and looking down on the concrete parking lot 100 feet below. The thought chilled her.

What about jumping onto subway tracks? Good probability. This dragged up the summer she'd taught English in Tokyo on the JET program. Commuting on the orange Chuo line in the orange sunset, she'd hear the announcement almost every day: "Someone has fallen from the platform at XYZ station. We're sorry for the delay; thank you for your patience."

Erika wasn't surprised by the announcement but by people's faces. The 9-to-5 workers always rolled their eyes. They were stirred not because someone had just been killed, but because they had to waste their 20 minutes again. The dark-suited men rolled their eyes at anything. At the aged, at the disabled, at the pregnant, at the young, anyone who disturbed their sleep in a crowded car.

All right, next. Exsanguination. What, like, cutting your wrist? Pain: 3 stars. Preparation: 3, ugliness: 3, probability: 1. Merely 5 percent succeeded in dying by this method. Oh. Forget it.

Gas poisoning: with natural or propane gas you'd die from asphyxiation and that would be excruciating. But with carbon monoxide from auto exhaust, you could die peacefully, and your body would remain as it was. Ah, didn't the Kirsten Dunst character die this way in *The Virgin Suicides*? Preparation: you need a 150-inch tube and duct tape, and this, and that. Ugh. Not for her.

Drowning: you'd die from asphyxiation, and it'd be way more painful than you think. Better to have your limbs tied but for that you'd need a friend's help. A few drinks and sleeping pills help. Corpses would be spoiled. Erika thought of Virginia Woolf and Ludwig II of Bavaria and Osamu Dazai. Why did they choose this one?

Self-immolation: the alternative name *bonzo* derived from the Japanese word 凡僧: *bonsou*, monk. Really? Folk-etymology. Pain: 5+, ugliness: 5+. Excruciating *and* you'd stay conscious. Sometimes you'd stay alive even if 100 percent of your skin surface was burned. And what if you survived?

Eeew.

Asphyxiation, starvation, electrocution—no no no no no. A firearm, she doesn't have. .

To freeze yourself: pain, 2; ugliness, 2. First you'd just shiver, and then by rectal temperature 35°C, you'd feel dispirited and sleepy. By 33°C to 32°C your vision would blur. By 30°C to 26°C you'd fall unconscious and that would be the end. If you managed to stay lower than 25 °C for long enough, you wouldn't survive.

Okay, this sounded good.

Erika scrolled to the bottom of the website. A screaming red banner was there: WINTER CLEARANCE, all women's apparel 60% off.

That's why Erika is here today. To get frozen. She'd been to this quiet beach long ago when her daughter was small. They had grabbed Subway sandwiches from nearby and strolled around for a nice spot to picnic when they happened to find the slope that led to this hidden arch.

It was a scorching sunny day. Or was it just the bottled sun in her memory?

Now it's 3:50 p.m., -10 °C, it feels. Soon the sun will set and the temperature will drop.

She has dawdled for about an hour. A sudden gust blows in her face and she cringes. She wraps herself up against the refrigerating wind. Skeletal trees along the shore dance.

Her stomach roars. She hasn't eaten anything today so that she wouldn't feel warm, or would feel tired, or feel or not feel whatever. Shouldn't she feel stuffed to get sleepy in the coldness? Her stomach roars again. She thinks of the Subway outlet around the corner. To distract herself, she observes a seagull awash.

"Erika?" A man's voice pops up from behind her. "What are you doing here all by yourself?"

Startled, she turns around. A plump balding man stands there. "Oh, Andrew," she says in her best cool voice. "You scared me. What are *you* doing here?"

Andrew is a man she knows from her badminton club in Burlington. She hates the club. True, it's a good club. Some play in the national league, but so what? Erika isn't bad either. But young blondes wouldn't play with her. They aren't any better; where does that attitude come from? It's a *club*, literally. *Boring*-ton, Erika would sniff. Male players are slightly better. Andrew is the best in the club.

"I'm going to pick up my daughter in St. Catharines." Andrew's chin is always tipped up to the left, as if the whole world makes him wonder. The cold has reddened his ears. "I just felt like dropping by. We used to come here often, me and my daughter. When she was like, a toddler."

So, it's not my secret garden, thinks Erika, mildly disappointed.

"May I?" Andrew pulls out a crumpled cigarette pack from his back pocket. "Did you want one?"

Erika hasn't smoked for about 20 years. Why not? Don't they all want a smoke before they die in films?

Andrew lights her cigarette. "It's my birthday today, turning," he says, puffing out a thread of smoke. "Forty-three."

"Oh, I'm 43 too," she says, her voice raspy.

"Get out. I thought you were 33."

"You can always add 10 when you guess an Asian woman's age."

"We're going to Boston Pizza to have some beer. Wanna join us?"

Erika blinks. "Boston Pizza? Why Boston Pizza?"

Andrew tilts his head to the other side. His expressive eyes are saying Why not?

"I mean," Erika mumbles, "it's your birthday, isn't it? I mean— Boston Pizza's good but why don't you go downtown? If you want pizza, I know a fabulous pizzeria on the Ossington strip."

Erika's mind drifts. She loves that neighbourhood: Ossington Avenue, Dundas Street, College Street. There's also this stylish bistro, Japanese-French fusion, where you can taste a variety of wines with chopstick dishes. Erika's mouth waters. *I definitely have to go there again.*

Andrew is still silent.

Erika begins to feel nauseous because of the smoke in her empty stomach. She smoothes over it.

"Are you OK?" he says. "Wanna have some water?" He conjures up a plastic bottle. "It's not opened. You can keep it."

She sips the Life Brand water. It tastes almost sweet. It soothes her throat and seeps into her stomach. Oh, she remembers, she has a $10 Shoppers' coupon. It expires next week.

He watches her drink. The wind has stopped. The sky is now orange.

"Better?" he asks.

St. Clair West

"Darn it," Joonsung muttered. His fingers were trembling above *The Economist* spread open on his lap. "Can't do this."

Yukari was sitting on the bed by the wall, opposite him, watching him roll a joint with a sheet of Zig-Zag. Dry leaves fell from between his stout fingers. He licked the edge of the paper, sealed it, and twisted the tip.

He lit the joint, put it in his mouth and pursed his lips. He didn't puff on it; instead, he inhaled deeply.

"Good stuff," he said.

Passing it to her, he began to chuckle to himself. "Did you see the note on the door?" He took on a female voice. "Joonsung, your *frend* Michael dropped by," he said, and burst out laughing. "'Friend' without 'i.' That Portuguese landlady can't even spell the simplest word!"

Yukari didn't get what was so funny about it, but Joonsung was a bit drunk. She puffed on the joint a few times and looked out the window. Orange sodium-vapour streetlights came into the narrow bedroom. It was a student residence. Where? She didn't know. St. Clair West, she thought he'd said to the cab driver.

The orange streetlights reminded her of the day she'd first arrived in Toronto. It had been November the previous year. From the airplane window she'd gazed down at the orange dots that seeped through beneath thin clouds.

On her way to her apartment at Islington, streets were covered with snow. The cold air pricked her cheeks. She'd pulled herself together and braced herself for a new life.

Yukari had come to Toronto from Tokyo to learn English. In Tokyo, she was an *OL*—"office lady" in "Engrish"—at a large microscope manufacturer, and having an affair with her boss who was married with children. That was what you got for a *tandai*, a women's college degree in Japan, if you had just graduated. Kinky sex once a month, in a two-hour session at a "love hotel," with a merry-go-round waterbed and a gynecological exam chair. After the play, he'd immediately put on his white dress shirt as if nothing had happened. She'd look at his back in silence.

What's wrong with having affairs? her colleagues would ask. This simulates the future, Yukari. In a few years we'll get married and quit the company and become housewives. Enjoy affairs so you'll learn how our future husbands will cheat on us. Enjoy free meals at top restaurants and fancy gifts from your guy because we work so hard for little money to wipe men's asses. But when her boss got her a Louis Vuitton handbag, a souvenir from his business trip to Hong Kong, she said that was it. She quit the firm and grabbed a ticket to Toronto. She was 22.

During the first few months in Toronto, she learned English at a private language school. Her instructor was part Italian, part Greek, part Dutch and many other things, and soon he became her instructor in bed too. According to him she wasn't "short" but "petite." Her jet-black hair and almond eyes were "exotic." One day something "clicked" and they got "connected," but it seemed the bed sessions expired every second month, and when the new arrival came—a young Chinese girl—Yukari learned some more English phrases such as "moved on" and "no hard feelings," and "friends with benefits." Maybe Joonsung's landlady was right: a friend without an "i."

Joonsung took the joint back from her, inhaled, and held his breath. He leaned backward, tucking his arms under his head. The white back of his upper arms floated in the dimness of the room. No, they were more silver than white.

"You're so pretty, Yukari," he said. He'd been saying this since the first day they'd met. So, now we're going to do it, she thought. Ah, classic. The same old same old, a phrase she'd just learned that day.

He moved beside her and sat on the bed. He motioned her to lie down, wrapping his arms around her shoulders. "Relax," he said, slipping his cold hand into her T-shirt. After stroking her back gently for a while, he pulled his hand out. He began to stroke her forehead. "Good night," he said. It was 2 a.m.

"You're pretty," he said again the following morning in the cafeteria on the fifth floor of OISE. *As if,* she said to herself in that newly-learned phrase, sipping nutty-flavoured coffee from a paper cup. Joonsung and Yukari were taking the same English Learning Program. They were the only East Asians in the advanced class. She was glad she'd learned some English before she came to Canada so she didn't end up in the intermediate class, which was full of Asian students who always stuck together in the cafeteria, talking to each other in their own languages, dreaming about getting jobs in multinational corporations when they returned home.

"Can I ask you something?" she said to him while they were standing in line at the checkout. "Why didn't we do it last night?"

"I was ready," he said, and smiled. "But you weren't."

She didn't understand what he really meant. Not ready? She wanted to laugh if he thought she was a virgin. Her turn to pay came. A toonie clinked on the countertop.

She stepped aside and, sipping her coffee, waited for him to pay for his items. Joonsung was tall and well-built for an East Asian. He'd completed his military service in his country. A quiet, untalkative man, she thought about him at first, just because he was Asian. A non-flirting man, unlike many Japanese men. But those *you're prettys*. As if.

"You don't have to act like a western guy just because you are learning English, Joonsung," she'd said to him when he'd first said that to her.

"Yukari, you pronounce my name perfectly," he'd said. "Everyone here calls me Johnson."

"Johnson? It's like, not even a first name."

"I don't care."

"You pronounce my name perfectly too, Joonsung." Many people wanted to call her Yuka, but since Yuka alone could stand as another Japanese name, she protested. So they called her Kari.

Their classmates were fun people. Several Europeans and even a Quebecer. Among the English learners the word or phrase of the week was always going around. Once a student started to overuse some expressions, it affected the others too. There were weeks of "fed up" and "uncool" and "classic." "Shenanigans" was everyone's favourite for a long time.

The OISE fourth floor, where their classrooms were, was a sanctuary for newcomers. Everything was ready for them: parties at Madison's, one-day trips to Niagara, tickets for the Jays' games. But Yukari and Joonsung decided to create their own activities.

When they learned that Yonge was in *The Guinness Book of World Records* until 1999 as the longest street in the world, they rented a car and drove north on it, hoping to reach its end. They went to see stand-up comedy and Shakespeare in High Park, even though they were only able to understand half of the performances. But everything was fun. He didn't want to hang out in Koreatown like other Korean students. "I have only one year here," he'd say. "I'm going to do everything Canadian, not Korean."

Once when they were taking a walk on Bloor, they ran into a couple in front of the Manulife Centre. It was Yukari's former language teacher and a woman, probably a South Asian. They stood arm in arm. She was smiling, but he seemed to be shocked. So this is his new lady, thought Yukari. She knew where they were heading: the Panorama. She even knew what he might have said to the woman: I'll take the most beautiful woman to the most beautiful bar in town. We must go in there, arm in arm, so we will look like a couple.

Same old same old.

Joonsung noticed the tension. Without saying anything, he reached out and put his arm around Yukari's shoulder.

The morning air got cooler, and the days got shorter. Autumn was coming. Yukari's study permit would expire in a couple of months. She began to wonder about her life after this. Most Japanese students she'd gotten to know had gone back to Japan. Did they get the jobs they wanted? They at least had goals. Yukari realized that she didn't have any. She'd just fled. From her work, from the male-dominated society, from a relationship that led nowhere.

She enjoyed life in Toronto, but she'd been feeling that she hadn't made the most of her stay. Her English was probably now good enough to find a job in a multinational corporation in Japan, but perhaps not good enough to work in Toronto. After all, she was still a pampered student on the OISE fourth floor.

Joonsung had decided to apply to a Canadian college for the next year against his parents' wishes and was taking a TOEFL preparation course. "I'll do anything Canadian," was still his favourite phrase. "I'm not like other students who have just come here to add 'overseas experience' to their resumes, which is required to get jobs in big corporations in my country. I'm not going to take preparation courses forever and take TOEFL or TOEIC every single time, like others, to get high scores. I'll give myself just one chance, and I'll get the required score."

Joonsung's willpower was almost too much for her. Their romantic relationship didn't seem to develop either. Koreans had mild disdain for premarital intercourse, so she had heard from some women, but she wasn't sure if that was true.

Thinking about him, she went into a Korean grocery store on Bloor West. The sweet smell of crispy, freshly baked *taiyaki*, or fish-shaped Japanese pancake, filled the store. On the community pin board she saw a poster: *Colour up your life*. It was a flyer for a beauty school. The dark-complexioned face of a woman was in the centre of it, metallic yellow and fuchsia pink applied on her upper eyelids, vermillion on her lips. Yukari had never seen such a colourful image before. In Japan, the makeup code for decent women was pearly beige, baby pink, and light ochre. Looking at the flyer, she remembered what her former classmate, a middle-aged Taiwanese lady, told her: I'm signing up for a beauty school. You can extend your study permit, and even get a diploma from Ontario. Most colleagues will be *real* Canadians and you can learn *real* English. You know, Yukari, it's so multiracial here, we could learn ethnically correct makeup. That's something we can't do in Asia, isn't it? Girl, time to get out of the OISE fourth floor.

Joonsung's phrase crossed her mind: I'll do anything Canadian.

Yukari tore off a strip with the school's telephone number and URL from the bottom of the flyer.

Later that night, when she was about to check the website, she found a familiar name in her inbox.

It was her former boss in Japan.

He couldn't know my new email address, she thought. She clicked it open.

It's me, it started. I asked Kawada-san for your new email address. So sorry if I startled you. How have you been? Your English must be so perfect now.

Creepy, she thought. Yet she couldn't close the window. Her thoughts drifted.

Mr. Miyabe was his name. He was 16 years older than her. Slim as a pencil, his fingers like noodlefish. Grasseater, her colleagues would call him secretly, making fun of his herbivore-like big eyes. She knew that he was always looking at her, stealing glances at her from between the papers piled on either side of his desk, over the computer screen, through a trail of steam rising from his coffee mug—watching. One night at a usual after-work drinking session in which everyone had to participate, she felt tipsy, and he brought her home by cab. This was how it started. Classic.

At first, she enjoyed his spending money on her. For the first time she felt as if she was one of the popular colleagues who were always in the chicest outfits, checking out the coolest hangouts in town with their men's money. Mr. Miyabe would tell her how his wife, a lawyer, was mean to him, not treating him right, making him feel small. He'd whine, putting his hands on Yukari's breasts, like a cicada hanging from the trunk of a pine tree, saying how Yukari was nice and warm and soft. Pity, she'd felt. Yes, at least at the beginning, but at some point, it had turned into love, she now recalled. Love. That was why that Louis Vuitton embittered her so much.

Or was it his silence that killed their love? When they were caught, his wife called her a bitch. All of this wouldn't have happened if you hadn't spread your legs, bitch. He's been such a faithful husband, he couldn't have even imagined cheating on me. I'm going to sue you.

Yukari had looked at him. He gazed off and didn't say anything. His wife's triumphant smile was like a sad victory.

Speechless, Yukari showed his wife the texts on her smartphone. Yukari, sweetheart, you know my dragon wife is going on a weekend trip with her friends. Yukari, my love, you could probably come over to my place and we could watch the Brad Pitt movie you wanted to see …

Anyway, I have a very important matter to discuss with you. Actually, I'll be in Toronto next week. We could meet, yes?

In the lobby of a business hotel near Union Station, she saw a bald forehead in a white Uniqlo down vest waving at her. Oh my goodness, he's getting chubbier, she thought.

"You haven't changed at all, Yukari!" he said, bowing like a stranger. "Thank you for coming to see me today."

Sunk deeply into a sofa, he began to leaf through his guidebook with his slim fingers. Neon yellow sticky notes rustled as he turned the pages. "Let's go to The Hockey Hall of Fame, Yukari. And to the CN Tower, of course. How about the Aquarium?"

"Well, I've already been to all those places," Yukari said. "It's all a bit pricey and I'm not so thrilled to go again."

"Don't worry, my company's going to pay for everything."

Looking at his fish-like fingers, she thought of the long drive on Yonge Street and afternoon walks on Bloor. It was still warm for the end of September, and the perspiration on his forehead seemed slightly greasy.

"How about taking a walk?" she said.

He pinched his brows, tipping up his chin to the side. *Walking?*

They did the Hockey Hall of Fame and the CN Tower. At the end of the day, he asked her to choose the best restaurant for them to dine, but she picked a random beer pub somewhere on Queen West. She ordered locally brewed pale ale.

After a lot of small talk, he said he'd quit the microscope manufacturer and launched a new business specializing in the automobile interior. "Do you remember our Flex-Axis microscope heads? Did you know the technique is also used for in-vehicle infotainment controllers? Smart, yes? Anyway, I have a deal for you."

Deal?

"Now that I'm independent, I could hire you as my secretary. You are not just a pretty face—very organized and talented. You'd get your own office next to mine, you know, private."

Ah, same old same old.

"I'm *fed up*," Yukari said in English, standing up from the stool. "I've *moved on*." She continued to speak English.

Ignoring his puzzled face, she threw a 10-dollar bill on the table and left the pub.

Yukari waited for the streetcar that was supposed to be there. "I've been waiting for Queen streetcars way too long in my life," said a lady behind her. Yukari took out her phone from her cross-body bag. She wanted to check out the website of the beauty school. She noticed a message flashing on the display.

I'm not making my one-year of "doing Canadian."

Joonsung?

What do you mean? she replied.

She waited for a response for as long as it took the streetcar to arrive. She threw a token into the box and went back to staring at her phone.

My study, a new window popped up. *I gotta go back to South Korea the day after tomorrow. My grandfather is in the hospital in critical condition. I'll have to help his business with my father for a while.*

Oh no, she voiced it, and then typed it.

But I'll try to come back here during the holidays. If … you'll still be here.

I've just found something Canadian to do, she wrote.

Good for you.

I think I'm ready, she wrote. *Can I come to your place?*

Sure thing.

The Queen streetcar was as slow as usual. It was getting hot and humid inside and started to smell like old snow boots. She jumped off at the next stop into the hot-dog smell that wafted from the corner stand. She grabbed a cab.

"St. Clair West," she said to the cab driver.

The Comedian

Nina's Saturday has begun just like the past three weeks. In the kitchen, she makes herself a bowl of Cheerios. It's a weekend, so she treats herself to a jar of blueberry yogurt. She twists the lid off and licks the smear.

It's 3 p.m. Chloe is picking her up soon. It's darkening outside. There's a rumble in the distance. *Thunder spoils milk*, her Granny would say. Having lived in Canada for half a century, she never forgets German sayings. Nina empties the rest of the milk into a glass and drinks it up.

Chloe and Nina have arrived at the Bavarian Forest Restaurant in Kitchener. The pink neon sign, of which only the "Forest" part remains, buzzes feebly.

This is their fourth gig at the Bavarian Forest as dancers. A singer and a comedian are also part of the team. Today, instead of Dave, there's a new comedian. But they aren't surprised. Comedians come, comedians go. Singers come, singers go. Backstage, Chloe and Nina put on their Rio-the-Carnival costumes. Nina puts a tiara on her head. A slight headache has already begun.

The air in the restaurant is stagnant, like that of the Amazon rainforest. Offstage Nina sees the singer humming, pearls of perspiration on her forehead. Chloe and Nina come onstage from either side, eyeing each other with pasted-on smiles. The rhythm doubles. Samba. The scent of Chloe's coconut oil lingers in the air, and Nina thinks of her piña colada at the Copacabana. The red-cheeked old men behind the beer steins catapult their arms into the air, smartphones in their hands.

That's okay. People staring at Nina know that she is a dancer. She *is*, not she *wants to be*. Just like she *is* a woman, *is* 25, *is* Canadian. She *is*, even though she isn't on Broadway, in Kitchener.

That's why she doesn't have a day job. Because she is a dancer. For Granny it isn't an occupation. Every day since she'd left college, Granny put a blue Post-it on the door of her room: "What are you going to do with your life?" When she was about to go on a Contiki tour through South America—unlike most of her friends who took grand European tours—the note read: "You want to die before you live?"

In the hall, Nina finds Chloe sitting on a young man's lap, still in her Rio dress. A large, rugged hand is petting her belly.

"Oh, hey," she says, looking at Nina, labouring to smile.

Yes, Nina knows this. If only this wasn't two hours away from home, she'd let her go with him. But she can't. She wants to go back home. "*Er*—I'm ready to go."

"Sure, yeah."

"Hey," a calm, deep voice pops up from behind Nina. She turns around. There stands the comedian. She sees him better now that he's without his makeup. Well into his thirties, his hair a straight dark blond, his eyes green, his lips thin. "If you need a ride, I could take you."

What other options does she have?

His Focus heads back to Toronto on the 401. It's begun to rain. Neither of them talks. All she hears is the *shush* of the tires. Suddenly he asks, "Where do you live?"

"Near the Runnymede station."

He doesn't answer. He looks into the rear-view mirror, squinting at the high beams from behind.

He turns on the radio. A female, country popstar is playing.

"Bitch," he mumbles. "I teamed up with her in Ottawa a long time ago." He glances sideways at Nina for a second. "Just for one night. She slept with the manager of the club and the next day we all got let go. She got her *happy-ever-after-solo-gig*."

Silence falls. *Ooh*, Nina says, in an almost inaudible voice.

"What are you up to tomorrow?" he asks.

She thinks about Sundays. Are they different in any way from Saturdays? She sleeps in, pours the rest of Cheerios into her mouth directly out of the box, eats chocolate bars. Mumbles to herself, gets drunk in the early afternoon, and watches random video clips on YouTube for hours. Oh, sometimes she smashes the Rio costume against the wall; what she doesn't do on Saturdays.

"Nothing special," she says. "You?"

"Me?" he says. "I'll cry."

"Cry?" She turns to him. "But … you're a comedian."

"So?" He shifts to the left lane and passes a car. "Crying is healthy." She doesn't know what to say.

"You wanna join me sometime?" he asks.

"Join what, crying?" Here you go. She squirms in her seat. She searches for the right words, just like when she brushes off someone at the bar counter after getting a free drink from him.

A green sign comes into sight, a heads-up for the junction ahead. "I live in Oakville, actually," he says.

"Why didn't you tell me?" she says, relieved at the changed topic. "I feel bad. Oh. You're going all the way to—"

"Not a big deal."

"It's a pretty little town, isn't it? Oakville."

"Yes, it is."

She wants to say something more about it, but she doesn't really know Oakville. "The lake—"

"You know what it's like at the end of Trafalgar?" He speaks over her. "Trafalgar's like Yonge Street to you guys, the busiest street in town. You drive south on Trafalgar and pass Lakeshore, and it dwindles and dwindles until it gets to the lake, and there," he says, going back to the right lane, "is a bench. Just a tiny little bench at the end of Trafalgar, looking down at the lake."

"And there you cry."

"Sometimes," he says. "Toronto's skyline makes me cry."

"How come?"

He muses for a while. "I guess I just want someone to take me out for a drink."

In front of her apartment, she half-turns to him, his face lit orange by the streetlights.

"Thank you," she says.

He gives a small nod.

"Maybe I'll join you sometime." She opens the door of the passenger seat. "One of these Sundays."

The Man Who Sells Clouds

When the hard rain begins, the train station, which was visible until a minute ago, disappears. The raindrops jump on the ground, and the lukewarm, petrol smell of asphalt is set free by the humidity. People on their way home make "Ugh" sounds and step off the street. Under the eaves of a drugstore, a young woman puts her red Ferragamo purse into a white plastic bag.

Ken tries to find a spot under the eaves of the nearest store which is already occupied by people who eye Ken and make faces, as if chasing a dog away. He proceeds to the next store and to the next, and the situation is the same. The last is a flower shop and he finds a small alley behind it. He becomes curious about where it leads. As he turns the corner, the scent of goldband lilies in front of the shop stings his nostrils.

Ken goes through the dark, narrow alley, passing three cerulean-blue garbage bins and comes to a dead end in a small courtyard with a yakitori stall. He sees the stooped shoulders of grey, black, and dark blue suits surrounding the counter. *If I sit among them, would I look the same?* he wonders.

Everything is dry in this courtyard, without any trace of rain. Ken looks up.

He sees the blue sky.

Noticing his puzzled face, one of the men sitting in the stall says to Ken, "Sit down here, young man."

Ken sits between a round-faced man in a grey suit and a grey-haired man in a black suit. "You're new here, aren't you? Surprised? Diego did it," says the same man to Ken, the round face, pointing first at the sky and next behind the stall. His moon face is oily and as shiny as his black, square-framed glasses.

Behind the stall, a small, dark-complexioned man sits on a straw mat, cross-legged as if in meditation. Paintings lean against the grey brick wall, visible from where Ken sits. They are all paintings of skies.

"Diego sells clouds," the grey-haired man says. His eyebrows are long and shaggy like a Miniature Schnauzer. "He's stopped the rain for us today, pro bono! You know, it was too sudden." He points at the sky like the other man.

This is weird. Ken wants to change the topic. "Are you guys always here, drinking?"

"Almost always," says a man with a yuzu-yellow tie sitting opposite Ken. "What are you going to do at home? As soon as I get home, my wife starts to follow me around, telling me what happened during the day. She follows me to the bathroom and tells me what Kitano Takeshi said on TV. I mean, I like Kitano, but when I come home after a long day, I just want to wash my hands and sit down and have a beer, that's all. I don't really care what Kitano said, you know? Women, why don't they understand?"

The yakitori cook has been quiet the whole while. He grabs five skewers off the grill, dips them into the teriyaki sauce, and lays them back on the grill. The skewers sizzle.

"Are you single, young man?" the round face asks, tilting his head away from the rising smoke.

"Sort of," Ken says.

"That's good!"

The men surrounding the counter cheer up. Ken sees the middle-aged men having fun with the thirty-something-year-old lost in the alley.

Long eyebrows nudges Ken in the ribs. "Go have a look at Diego." And then he wipes the dark-violet lump of old, dry soy sauce with his thumb off the mouth of a sauce bottle.

Ken stands in front of his straw mat.

"Hello," Diego says without looking up at him.

Ken looks around at the paintings. They all describe clouds. Whipped cream horns of cumulonimbus above a lake, a series of L-shaped cirrus over a steel bridge, scales of a sardine of cirrocumulus between coloured trees, an outflow boundary looking like Niagara Falls over the prairies, and a UFO-like, upside-down white plate of lenticular cloud above a mountain in the dark. The one at the left corner grabs Ken's attention. The terra-cotta horizon is about to suck the floating, golden cotton balls. The price for the painting is 20 thousand yen per 1km.

"That was May the 17th, 2010," Diego says, as if he was talking to himself. Ken doesn't understand what he means.

"I can reproduce any skies, whenever, wherever. I take orders too. It costs extra though."

Ridiculous, thinks Ken. Still, he asks, "Do you know what the sky looked like on June the 28th, 2008?"

"One moment. I'll check the archives." Diego opens the upper drawer of the apple-green celluloid cabinet he has been leaning on and starts to scan the copies of paintings with his root-like forefinger.

Archives, repeats Ken in his mind.

"Was it Tokyo?" Diego asks.

"Yes."

"Here you go. It was very fine the whole day. The first blue sky after rain for a month."

That is correct. It was Ken's wedding day. He remembers the day as if it was yesterday, for that is one of the most beautiful memories of his miserably ended marriage.

"Nobody trusts me at the beginning," Diego says, examining Ken's expression. "But I do sell clouds. I can drop some lightning at 4:23 p.m. tomorrow if you like. Where is your office?"

It is sunny and warm the next morning. Ken's suit from yesterday smells like burnt teriyaki sauce, so he decides to wear another suit for the day. He is so busy that he doesn't think of the oddities in the alley. However, at 4:23 sharp, from his desk at an insurance company, he sees lightning scribble down the darkening sky.

After work, Ken goes back to the alley. Seeing Ken come back, the men at the yakitori stall eye each other. "Welcome to the club," says today-again-yuzu-yellow tie.

Ken doesn't sit down at the stall and goes directly to the cloud shop.

"Diego," Ken says, panting. "I don't believe in coincidence, OK? Tomorrow, can you do a drizzle in the morning, a blue sky until three, and then snow?"

"I can do snow, but I won't. It's August. How about hail instead? From 5 to 5:10?"

The following day is exactly as Ken and Diego have arranged. Ken goes to see Diego again after work.

"You said you take orders, right, Diego? Can you change the past weather?"

"With an extra cost."

"Can you remove the thunder clouds from the sky of the Mount Ten area, August the 29th, 2009?"

"I'll go by train," Ken's wife said, ripping off coupons from a flyer at the kitchen table. "It's just three hours from Tokyo to Osaka. I know it's faster by plane, but think of the extra time for checking in, going to the airport."

"But it's five thousand yen cheaper with the last-minute offer," Ken said, smoothing down his wife's silky black hair. His wife was supposed to visit her family in Osaka with their 11-month-old daughter. When they'd got married, his wife was already at the end of her pregnancy. The baby who'd been born the previous summer had started to toddle.

"The little one wants to walk around, anyway. She'd be excited to be on the plane for the first 15 minutes and then she'd get bored. If I am to follow her around, it'll be easier to do so on the train than on the plane, don't you think?"

"But it's five thousand yen!" Ken said again.

"Oh well, what can I do with you?" his wife said.

When the negotiation with Diego is done, Ken starts to look forward to the following weekend. On Friday evening, he gets dispirited. *Maybe I'm up to something really silly.* On Saturday, though, he takes a train and leaves for Mount Ten, one hour north-west of Tokyo. The nostalgic box-seat cars make Ken feel as if he were going on an excursion. An old lady next to him is peeling a frozen mandarin orange.

At quarter to six, Ken is standing at the skirt of Mount Ten. It's August. The same hot summer weather as that day. It's muggy like a sauna and Ken feels sweat running down between his shoulder blades. A crickets' orchestra is fighting against a cicadas' rock band. A coupling pair of dragonflies is sinking down right and left as if they are *Awa* dancing above the yellowing rice fields.

It is supposed to be the reproduction of the sky of August 29th, 2009. However, as Ken has ordered, there isn't a single cloud in the sky. Only the endless gradation of blue behind Mount Ten. Ken marches through the white and powder-pink and magenta cosmoses, which are as tall as him, toward Mount Ten.

"A thunderstorm is coming," Ken's wife said, watching the weather report on TV the day before her flight. "I'm worried." She took a pen out of their daughter's mouth. The baby groaned for a while in protest.

"If it's really dangerous, they'd cancel the flight, right? If they don't, it should be fine, right?" Ken said optimistically.

Ken looks up to Mount Ten. There are no other mountains around it and its shadowy independent twin-peaks, like an upper lip, stand out against the deep marine-blue sky. Ken begins to wonder if this is really the reproduction of the sky on the appointed date.

Flight 439 departed on time despite a typhoon warning. Fifteen minutes after departure, the airplane crashed into Mount Ten. When he heard the news, Ken was lying lazily on the rug, watching TV and eating Cheetos. The news anchor repeated that it appeared no one had survived. *No one had survived*, Ken parroted in his mind. He sat up slowly. The white rug got orange stains from his fingers. He recalled conversations with his wife.

At five to six, as Ken is still gazing into the sky, a white airplane suddenly appears about a kilometre east of Mount Ten. He doesn't know how it has appeared. He tries to figure out which airline it is. He thinks he clearly sees the logo of the airline. *Yes, that's it. That's the flight my family is on*. Ken starts to run, following the plane.

He runs into the fields, pushing away cosmoses, chasing away dragonflies, and he runs, following the plane. It is not until his legs are caught by heavy mud that he realizes he has stepped into the rice fields and now he is stamping, like a sumo wrestler trying to make his way. The plane hides itself behind the peaks for five seconds. For Ken, this feels like five years. His breath is hot, gasping.

Ken sees the plane coming out from behind the peaks. *It's still there.* Ken resumes his chase. He runs as far as he has paid for.

On Monday, Ken visits Diego again.

"How did you like it?" Diego asks.

"Diego, can I buy the same sky again, for the next weekend?"

"With an extra cost," says Diego says, wiping dust off a painting with his root-like forefinger.

The Summer with No Mosquitoes

I'm about to make a left turn into the YMCA on Speers Road. The traffic light turns red. I hate this traffic light. It must be programmed to turn red whenever I'm here. The parking lot of the YMCA is filling with the cars of other moms who have just dropped off their kids at school. After circling three times, I find a spot.

Rushing in, I take my phone out of my pocket to check the time. 9:05. This is my life: always five minutes late. In the changing room I realize that I've accidentally brought a zebra-patterned push-up bandeau instead of a schoolgirl tankini. Shit. You're supposed to take a shower before entering the swimming pool, but I just pass through the area and open the door to the pool. In the water float white-haired heads bobbing up and down to the blaring Olivia Newton-John. A portly man in the corner throws a *woo-hoo* look at me. I shake my hands and head, pretending to be shivering after a cold shower.

On my way back from Aqua Fit, I pass along the glass panes to the gym and look inside. Now Step Fit is going on. Women in Lululemon tops step up and down the small, slim risers in front of them, jabbing their arms straight up in the air. Isn't this the right age group for me? Someone at the far end catches my eyes. It's an elderly Asian lady. Totally lagging behind, though not seeming to care, she steps up and down, slowly, with her arms up, elbows bent, as if she were holding a huge watermelon in the air. It reminds me of the Japanese *bon odori* dance at summer festivals.

The moon is out, out, the moon is out,
Over the coal mine, the moon is out, eh, eh ...

A month since I last visited the Y. So last month's membership fee is more like a donation. Would I get a tax credit for that?

The railroad crossing bell starts to clang and the boom gates descend. I hate this crossing. If it weren't there, my life would be much better. Ten-minutes better, at least.

Soon a huge shadow hurtles in front of us, giving a light quake to our car. "Look," I say, turning to the rear seat, "it's a GO."

"Oh, yeah?" my six-year-old son says, not looking up from his 3DS. I recall how not so long ago he got excited every time he saw GO trains, pointing and yelling, his eyes sparkling.

After dropping him off, I drive down to Speers and to the Y. When I arrive, it's well into the second half of the Aqua session. Afterward, I linger in the lukewarm leisure pool for another half hour. Then in the shower room I run into the Asian woman I saw a month ago. A petite lady with stooped shoulders, her hair cut short and blunt, wisps of grey cluster in front trimming her forehead. She seems Japanese to me, but who knows? Washing myself, I glance at her stealthily again and again, and see her drop her mini shower-gel bottle. "Ah," she says. I knew it; she's Japanese. That was a Japanese *Ah*. In the changing room I walk up to her and say "Konnichiwa," with a slight bow.

"Konnichiwa," she answers.

Her name is Kayo. She moved to Canada three years ago to live with her daughter who's married to a Canadian man with Jamaican heritage. The couple goes to work during the day, so Kayo takes care of her fourth-grade grandson after school and prepares meals. The men don't really like her cooking though, she says. "The only thing they like is Japanese curry," she says calmly and half smiles. She happens to be from Fukuoka City in Kyushu, where the moon song I associated with her the first time I saw her in Step is supposed to have originated. I tell her that her movements reminded me of the *bon odori* dance. Her smile widens, fine lines fanning out around her eyes.

My children and I moved into a corner unit of a row of townhouses, on a ravine lot, two months ago. Oakville is an expensive city to live in, but I wanted to stay close to their father. Though a decent shopping plaza is only a five-minute drive away, our backyard is like a provincial park. A brook meanders through it, fireflies wink at night. Fireflies! How I longed as a child to see this beloved image in my homeland. When I was ten, my mother died, and she left me a purple handkerchief which was coarse and rather like a beverage coaster, embroidered with beautiful fireflies, but I had never seen them in Tokyo. I had to wait until I was forty years old and living in a ravine in Oakville, Ontario.

I do some pharma patent translation and work from home. *You're lucky you can be home with kids and work*, friends say. *Why would you need day care?* I want to laugh.

I work at night when my kids are asleep. Maybe because of an odd biorhythm, I sleep light. Sometimes I doze at my desk, my brain untethered at last from the last sentence of translation. But in the early morning, I find myself with my bare feet on the dew-soaked deck facing the woods, my coffee warm on the wicker table beside me. The trees touch the pink sky. I stretch my arms out to their tops, my ears attune to the language of the wind, my nose to the damp leaves, my eyes to the green. Deer appear from nowhere, from out of the mist.

"Did you kill it?" my daughter asks, her tone is faintly teasing.

I rip off a piece of paper towel and pinch the dead mosquito on my forearm.

"*Eeew*," my son says, looking at the red stain on the paper. "Didn't you say killing is no good?"

"Mosquitoes are okay to kill."

"Why? You can't kill cats."

I try to recall what I have read in a recent book written by a young German philosopher. "Cats *think* so you can't kill them. Mosquitoes don't."

I hate mosquitoes. Just one of them, just one of these tiny little insects in your bedroom can ruin your night. With my sore eyes, I look at the clock. "Come on, let's go, we are running late!"

After dropping them off, I stop by an indoor playground and pay for the birthday-party package for my son. And then I drive to another plaza and buy some toys and trinkets for loot bags, and order nut-free cupcakes. The day has just started and I've already spent 350 dollars. Seriously, have I ever thrown a 350-buck birthday party for myself?

It's 10 a.m. Tuesday. If I rushed to the Y, I might catch up with Kayo after Step.

I turn the car key in the ignition, buckling up at the same time, and start off. This is my life: always slightly speeding. Fifteen minutes later, I am there. Among the ladies walking toward the changing room, I find her. Seeing me, she smiles, her cheekbones rise and narrow her eyes, making them two downward crescents. I smile too.

Kayo was born in 1940. She grew up in a suburb of Fukuoka, about 150 kilometers north-east of Nagasaki. It was—and still is—the biggest city in Kyushu, the southernmost island of Japan's four main islands. The coal mining village in the moon song wasn't too far, in the same prefecture, but "The song wasn't originally for the dance," she says.

Kyushu men back then were alpha males, females were house servants, but her father was rather a gentleman. Unlike many men of the time, her father had a grad school degree, which only made things harder for him. In a small town like theirs, there was no room for an overeducated person. He found a job at a local post office, but couldn't put up with his boss who was neither older nor more educated than he. Soon he found another job at a tailor, but he was too old to do an apprenticeship. Nothing lasted long.

Her mother was much younger. It was his second marriage and her first. In good times she wore a quaint kimono and had her hair set in a traditional, towering beehive every other day.

Her father ended up in pig farming and made his living selling sows. He was able to be his own boss that way. The business went okay. Kayo's parents were not necessarily well off, but they covered the fees for school excursions for poor coal vendors' children, or invited young teachers from Kayo's school for dinner.

Kayo liked their little farm. In the blue of the early morning, under the dim light of the naked bulb in the stable, she fed piglets. Sometimes she soaked her fingers in milk and let the piglets suck on them, feeling the tingle at the tips of her fingers. No matter what time of the day it was, there was always a certain early-morning quality. It was cool and shady with a whiff of hay and bird feed. She kept walking around, her booted feet roiling the muddy soil. Outside scurried a pair of black-tailed Japanese bantams. Their chicks snuck into the kitchen and cheeped and raced on the earthen floor. Then one day, they disappeared overnight. Paw prints of a fox were on the ground.

The early-morning fog would bring a sunny day, so said Kayo. I look out the window facing the ravine. The fog has lifted and dissipated, and I see leaves patter, flickering silvery. It's before noon and it's already getting muggy. Now I have to drive down to the lake to have lunch with a friend.

Down by the lake at the boat club it's breezy yet scorching. White waves curl far out in the lake beside the tiny lighthouse. Boats rock at the dock, their mainsails tipping toward the west in the wind. In front of the main doors she stands, my friend, a member of the club, waving at me with a free hand, a large paper bag from the Apple store in the other hand, smiling, her blond hair shining. She invites me in. We walk through the narrow hallway beside the empty restaurant, she nodding to the service staff and greeting other members. We come to the outside patio. In the swimming pool, five, six children under school age paddle on duck-shaped rubber boats watched by teenage lifeguards while adults have cocktails poolside. The walls of the clubhouse are a sharp white against the blue sky.

She orders a pomtini, I, a lemonade.

She has a sip of her drink. "This is definitely the best early-afternoon cooler. You should try it," she says, putting her water-beaded, long-stemmed martini glass back onto the table. The glass-top clinks. "So, how are you settling in, Ayako?"

"Fine," I say.

The smell of french fries wafts in the air from the clubhouse.

"You look tired," she says.

"I couldn't sleep well last night. It was a full moon. I can't sleep well with a full moon."

"What, are you a werewolf?" she says, and titters.

We eat salad with chicken strips. After that, she starts to take things out of the shopping bag. She will be taking a computer graphic course during the summer. "You're supposed to have a Mac," she says, raising her brows, holding her brand new laptop. And then takes out another package to open. And another.

A girl in the swimming pool tosses a yellow beach ball high into the air, against the blue sky.

The moon swims into my mind, the full moon over the coal-mining village, like a silent film. In the silence the little girl—now Kayo—pantomimes and feeds piglets with her fingers. *The moon is out, out, the moon is out.* When did I last see films—except ones by Pixar and DreamWorks and Disney—at all? I don't even remember. A huge black Japanese bantam flap in front of my eyes.

"Ayako?" she asks. "Are you okay?"

"Yes. Sorry."

"I just asked if you'd care for another drink. Or dessert, perhaps?"

I look at my watch. Two hours till I have to pick up my kids.

"I think I gotta go," I say.

I drive hurriedly to a Korean grocery store in Mississauga and buy some *taiyaki*, fish-shaped Japanese waffles with a sweet bean-paste filling, and then head back to Oakville to the Y. There is an afternoon Step session that I was once thinking of joining—and there she is. "I've got some *taiyaki* for you, Kayo-san," I call out, raising the brown paper bag.

She cracks a winning smile. I suggest we stay inside the air-conditioned cafeteria, but she wants to go outside. We walk to the back of the building to a cozy little nook on the undulating hill where summer camps for children will soon be held. We sit on the sun-baked, colour-drained lawn. I lie on my back and sprawl, feeling the spiky grass under the length of my limbs, and bask in the sun. Tiny flies swivel over lawn daisies. Birds warble, crossing the sky in a stream.

Kayo looks down on the fish-shaped waffle happily, splits it in half with her wizened hands, and bites into it on the tail side. Crumbs fall onto her lap. I offer my purple handkerchief. Her eyes widen.

"Where did you get this?" she asks.

"From my mother. She died when I was ten," I say. "I love this handkerchief. It's not soft at all, but I like it."

"Beautiful," she says. "Yes, it's hard, but this is silk. Hakata fabric. From Fukuoka." She touches the firefly embroidery. "It's usually used for obi sashes. I didn't know they make handkerchiefs too."

"Really. No wonder it's so coarse."

We laugh.

"On a sunny day like this," she says, "when I was a girl—I would stare down at my own shadow, count to twenty without blinking, and look up at the sky and find the shadow there. It was me of course, the shadow, but I decided to think it was my father's, when he was drafted."

The birds are black dots in the sky. Kayo looks down again.

The time took on a darker hue. It was 1945. Her father had long been serving, and finally her much older brother was conscripted. It fell to little Kayo to take care of the pigs with her mother, now in tattered cotton knickerbockers and her hair tussled, no more big hair and flowing robes. The pigs were sold one by one and were almost all gone. A strange quietness filled the stable. No hens that laid eggs, no feline animals on the prowl.

Finally, they had to sell the last sow. Maru was her name. It was June, sunny and sweltering. A break in the rainy season. Kayo gave Maru her last meal. She bleated throatily, as if she had been aware of her fate. Kayo touched the pig's boney back, ran her fingers along each protruding knob. "So long, Maru," she said.

Her mother left for the market with the pig. Kayo stood on a hill, gazing off in the direction of the city. The sky was turning gloomy. Plumes rose beyond the river, black dots gathered over it. Soon she heard a siren.

Spiders, flies, mosquitoes. You can find all kinds of bugs in this house. Ants. I keep the screens shut but they all work their way in. A big fat fruit fly crosses in front of my eyes lazily, as if it were mocking me. As I wring a duster in a washbasin, I hear an unfamiliar noise from downstairs. Among the rattle of the dishwasher, there's some kind of raking sound. Alarmed, I go downstairs and follow the noise. It's coming from the kitchen. On the granite top of the kitchen island, I see the plastic container of cupcakes that I've just picked up—moving.

Something pops up from behind it.

It's a grey squirrel.

Startled, it dives off the island, kicking the plastic container off the top. The container has fallen upside down. The squirrel scampers around, squeaking, and streaks off toward the screen to the outside deck. There is a big hole in the screen.

I grab the Swiffer stick and brandish it frantically in all directions. "Out, OUT!" I scream. "Get out!"

Panicked, the squirrel cannot find the hole that it has made itself. Standing up on its rear feet, it scratches the screen all over. I open the screen and it jumps out and runs away into the woods. I pull the screen shut with a bang. As I pick up the container, it opens with a plastic *click* and all the cupcakes fall, the yellow icing smearing the floor.

This is it. Enough of the Thoreauvian life.

Vexed, I rush to the Y. Kayo and I are supposed to have a picnic. Upon seeing me she asks, "Are you all right?"

"I meant to bring some cupcakes for you, but …"

"That's fine, dear."

We sit on the grass. Just then, a mosquito settles on the back of my hand. I see it and feel my cheek blush. I raise my other hand high, palm wide open, fingers spread.

"No! Don't!"

Kayo holds me by the wrist. I stare at her questioningly. She averts her eyes from mine saying sorry and lets my arm go. The mosquito has gone.

"That day—" she starts and pauses on a word. And then begins her story.

That day when her mother went to town to sell the pig, she didn't come home. The air raid had started, and she was stuck and couldn't get out of town. She found refuge in the basement of the National Fifteen Bank in the Hakata quarter, one of the appointed bomb shelters. Soon after midnight, the power went down, the doors got stuck, and people were locked in. The water pipes that were heated by the fires exploded, sending boiling water flooding into the basement.

Sixty-two people boiled in the water.

One of them was her mother.

Kayo had become one of the country's 120,000 war orphans.

It was June 1945.

Later that summer there were no mosquitoes in her village. The flames, the same flames that boiled the water with the sixty-two people, boiled all the water—the water in the pipes, in the rivers, in the ponds, in the pools of rain, until it boiled the last single larva.

Nagasaki was August, says Kayo. She looks up at the sky.

And she says: Sure we talk about Nagasaki. But we don't even talk about Tokyo where 10,000 lives were lost. Who would remember Fukuoka where only 1,000 were killed?

But I remember the summer, the summer with no mosquitoes.

It was quiet. A quiet summer.

Back at home, I find an ant on the kitchen floor tracking the icing left there. I pull out a flyer from the pile of papers, fold it in half and make a crease, and scoop the ant up. I slide the screen open and release it into the ravine.

What the Ant Said

It's 2 p.m. on a Tuesday afternoon and I'm still in bed. The smog alert chime rings. As if on cue I worm out of bed.

I look out the window. Highrises, chimneys, cars—the same old view, grey and slightly askew. *The smog alert has been issued*, the same old, metallic female voice echoes from speakers behind a bread factory. The all-too-familiar noises I've grown up with.

In the kitchen I drink a glass of water. Water is one of the two things I allow myself to intake during the last moments of my life. The other is *konjac*, potato jelly. Someone, a professor or something, said this on TV: You could die if you only drank water for one week. You could die peacefully if you filled up your stomach with some konjac along with it; it is filling, yet it has almost no calories.

I loved the idea and decided to do it. I want to die. But I don't want to die writhing with hunger. Wasn't there someone who had survived a winter in a mountain by eating snow? I don't care. I'm used to believing what I want to believe. Konjac sounds ideal. I'm from Gunma prefecture, one-hour north of Tokyo, which is famous for konjac potato production. What could wreathe my death more beautifully?

I know how tasty konjac can be when it is cooked in fish stock with soy sauce, sake, and sugar. But I boil it in plain water to avoid adding extra calories. I feel dizzy. This is the fifth day. Two more days and I'm supposed to be dead. I'm not in my PJs or sweats, though. I'm wearing a pair of soft stretch denim pants and a blue flannel shirt that hardly gets crumpled. I still shave my face. I don't want to look dishevelled and wretched when I will be found dead. Standing, I eat some jelly. I chomp it like no one is watching. Without any seasoning, it tastes like a rubber eraser.

What's the point of staying alive? I say to myself, the same old question I've been asking for months, staring at the stain in the sink. Humans are stupid, the world is insane.

I come back to the window and look out. I close my eyes. I still see the town spreading below my eyes. I can see every single alley, tell what food joints are there, hear an old man sprinkling water on the blazing street, smell the asphalt. I see people's faces. I even know what they might be talking about. I was born and grew up here. This is my home. Japanese is the only language I speak.

But I'm not accepted as one of them. Never. I'm Korean and living in disguise. With a false name, a false family history.

I open my eyes. A jet-black raven perched on the balcony railing is staring at me.

I used to have a friend like me. She was born and raised here too, knowing only one language. Her mother was an undocumented immigrant from Thailand, and after she got caught, the court ruled that they both had to be deported. A professor or something at a university for rich kids said it was a right of a sovereign nation to control its citizens. Hadn't he heard the term "Sanctuary City?" Pro-fuck-sor. We are not mangoes; mangoes that are plucked and traded between countries just to be eaten when they are at their best. When mangoes get planted, they root, adjust, and grow. Mangoes get lives. But who would care about such lives, displaced and hidden in the shadows? When they are done taking advantage of us, they don't need us any longer.

The world is deteriorating. It's not worth living.

My lower back is still feeling the relief after the hours of lying down but I walk away from the window and trudge back to my bed. I dive onto it. And I roll.

It is peaceful, at least this part of the world, around my bed.

I'm not sleepy. Staring at the ceiling, I begin seeing black hinged doors. I hadn't noticed that they'd appeared.

Those doors are familiar.

I try to recall when and where I saw them. I remember seeing these doors long ago. When was it? Ah, that was because of my elementary-school sweetheart.

Every day we went home together after school and got to her house first. She lived in a large, wooden bungalow painted light blue and surrounded by the yard, that we would have seen only in American films and which seemed totally out of place in those Japanese suburbs. In front of her house, we would dawdle for ten minutes or so because I didn't want to leave. She would patiently wait for me to leave with some dismay in her eyes. Once I didn't know what to say and pretended to be excited about stepping on the train of ants that was passing in front of us, grinding them with my foot.

You'll be cursed, she said to me with disgust. Don't you know ants do that?

That night in my bed, I wrapped myself in a blanket from head to toe and wept. *Ants are going to curse me.* The thought was so gruesome I couldn't sleep until past midnight. The following night, again in bed, I created an imaginary Buddhist altar on the vast white of the ceiling I was staring at, to pray. It had layers of eight pairs of doors. I opened them one by one, slowly, timidly, and prayed to the god of ants.

Now in my bed, I see the same altar on the ceiling. Gosh, I've started seeing delusions. Good. I open the doors, one by one, just like I used to do. Slowly. Gingerly. To pray to the god of ants.

There appears a huge, pitch-black head of an ant.

Oh, is it you? the ant says. Long time no see.

I don't recall seeing it before. I'm sorry, I say anyway, for what I did when I was a kid. Will you forgive me?

Oh, you mean those workers you killed, those who were prowling around the nest, the ant says. Never mind. Those were old ones. Old lives are useless, you know.

Wow, I say. I didn't know ants are ageist.

Of course, the ant says. When you are younger, you raise your children. My children, I mean, because only I am supposed to give birth in my clan—theoretically. And when you are old, you go outside and face danger. You'll soon die anyway. No workforce wasted here.

Make sense?

So, I say. You are the Queen.

Yes, yes, I am, it says, with a hint of conceit in its voice. What are you?

Me? I'm nothing. I'm just an office worker, if that's the answer to your question.

Hmmm, it says, you are so young and you are a worker. Humans are strange. And why the hell have you been lying there for days?

Oh, you've been watching me, I say, surprised. I'm just trying to quit living.

That's a very odd thing to hear, it says. You humans are funny. You'll die one way or another, why make the effort?

I don't want to wait, I say. My life is fucked up.

I hear the raven cry. I turn my head toward the window.

I say: When I got this job in my company, one of the biggest in this country, I was on top of the world. Stupid me—I've been working more than a 100 hours' overtime a month the last 15 months, with no days off and no extra pay, slapped and spanked like dirty livestock. And I made a minor mistake ... with my head heavy and my sight dim, I made a mistake. And I lost my job. My boss—a 50-year-old-codger still in the low and low in middle management, that loser—tortured me, verbally and physically, for two long hours, and in the end, he called me, blowing smoke in my face, a Chong ... a Chong ... I don't know how he found out but that's what he called me ... and I lost the job.

Anyways.

I shake my head and look at the ant again. You know what, I say, there was a woman like me in another company who took her own life. I saw the news on TV. A pro-fuck-sor said that it had been silly of her to commit suicide just because of overworking. And know what was funnier? The court ordered this company to pay only five hundred thousand yen for labour practice violations. Five hundred thousand! Our lives are like ants'! Oops, sorry.

That's a stupid system, the ant says. Middle management? We don't need such a hierarchical structure to run our organization. That would make everything unnecessarily complicated and there would be a lot of loss and waste.

But they have you, Queen. Aren't you the top of the organization that gives your workers orders?

Me? No. I'm just a childbearing machine. I don't even need to know what my workers are doing. Taking care of my babies, I suppose. And looking for food, of course.

So how do you manage to control the masses?

Control? We don't control anything. We are programmed to react. Don't you know our roles are determined by the time of our births? You don't *learn* anything; that's a myth. You just do what you are imprinted to do.

That's not true, I say. Even though I hated my work, there was something I learned and became better at. I can make better Power Point presentations than anyone else, I'm sure.

Ha! Get over yourself! the ant says. You are replaceable, you know that. No one will care when you are gone. You are just a tiny nothing to society.

I feel offended. I stare at the ant.

Oh, are you mad at me? The ant laughs. Like I said, everything is programmed. Your work. Your life. So is your social class. Everything is determined by birth. You can never become anything else.

That's stupid, I say. You guys are stupid.

No, humans are stupid. What matters is not you, but society! A collective world. Our society is our only interest. Each individual is like a sunflower seed, replaceable and unworthy. Even a spore knows that. Did you know they also shape society?

But that contradicts, um, evolutionary theory, doesn't it? I say, trying to keep my cool. We all want to pass on our genes to the next generation. Personal interests surpass society's.

Oh, no no no ... the ant says. If something is for society, it's for individuals too, eventually. It's nothing like self-sacrifice or anything, you understand? We stay collective so we can pass even more genes to future generations.

What do you mean?

You know, the ant goes on, all my children are sisters. In our species, at least. Are you familiar with genetics? We hymenopteran females have a pair of genomes, but our males have only one—simple, they are—

so female siblings share three-quarters of my genes. Why would my workers bother marrying men in order to create their own babies that would share only half of their genes? My keeping on providing sisters to them would be much more beneficial. Get it? Well, sometimes there are cheaters among workers who give birth to their own babies—but such babies, especially male ones, are usually removed and killed immediately by other workers. You see, our only interest is the eternal prosperity of our monarchy. Workers are under each other's constant surveillance; births are strictly controlled. To keep our blood. Pure, dense, strong female blood! Some queens of other species of ants can even clone babies. I like the idea; maybe I should give it a try too. Do you have a Mrs.?

Huh? The sudden change of the subject flabbergasts me. No, I don't.

Having said that, I think about Nan, the girl who was sent to Thailand. *I might have a picture of her. Where is it?*

You wanted to mate with her, eh? The ant says when I am about to get up.

Will you stop reading my thoughts? I say, vexed. No, nothing like that. She was a good friend.

You're lying. Of course you wanted to mate with her. What else is there between males and females? Reproduction is everything. That's why we create you males! That's the only meaning of your existence.

Don't you know there is a nobler, spiritual type of relationship? Friendship, we call it. If it's not love.

Friendship? Can we eat it?

Anyway, I say, with a dry feeling in my mouth. It tastes sandy. Like unseasoned konjac. I pause and mentally search for a cleverer thing to mention. Oh, yeah, bees, I finally say. I'm sure I learned at school that honeybees mate with different males to produce variations in genes. Aren't you both social insects? You guys sound far more backward.

Oh, those queen bees. They are sluts. They sleep with anyone and give birth to children from different fathers. Sluts and drones, what a combination. It seems to be working for them, though. The differences in genes create different reaction-thresholds; their workers can react to different tasks at different times, which seems to lengthen their colonies' lifespan.

Here we go, I say. That's what we appreciate in the humans' world. Differences. Diversity, we also say. Right after saying this to the ant, I ask myself: Do we really?

That's not necessary, the ant says, dismissive of what I have said. There are so many other ways to keep colonies thriving. Parasitism, conquest, slavery. Do you want to know what we do? Sometimes a queen invades a host colony and kills their queen and rubs the dead one's biofluid into her skin to disguise her smell; sometimes a worker kills a worker from the target colony and bites its head off and adopts it as a mask and uses its feelers to fool other workers. Sometimes ...

Stop it ...

Slavery. There is a slave-making species called Samurai-ant and their soldiers steal pupas from ...

Stop it!

Do you finally get it? Our world is better. Why don't you come over here? Cross the line to this side. To the better side.

Stop it! STOP IT! STOP. IT!

I rise abruptly, propping my upper body with an elbow, facepalming with the other hand.

I get out of bed. Dizziness strikes me and I have to crouch down, but I get up again.

Now I'm going downstairs to the convenience store on the ground floor of this apartment building, and I'll buy all the bento-box meals they have and eat them up. Those bentos they throw away hours before the expiration so their customers can always have plenty of fresh choices. Where is my wallet? It's been five days since I last used it, the day I bought dozens of konjac. I find it on the floor near the kitchen.

I open my front door.

"Hello," the cleaning guy says.

Swish, swish, his broom sweeps over the floor. I get on the elevator.

Swish, swish, the sounds still linger in the elevator when the doors close.

Nobu's Writing Therapy

Nobu Hamayama stands on the terrace in front of his bungalow looking up at the blue sky. Above him soar banana and papaya trees. Fruits hang from their branches and stems: his breakfast. Wayan walks to the trees. She climbs the ladder over the hibiscus, hibiscus that has grown as high as Nobu's height and higher, almost like small trees, red and pink and white. He has never seen hibiscus grow so high.

This is his second month in the town of Ubud on the island of Bali. He is a new branch manager of a Japanese trading company. From the terrace he sees Wayan, his secretary, plucking a bunch of bananas and a papaya. She climbs down the ladder, takes the fruit to the kitchen, and returns carrying a platter.

"Here you are," Wayan says, putting the fruit platter on the table.

"Thank you, Wayan-san," Nobu says.

"You're welcome, Hamayama-san."

"Just call me Nobu."

On this Hindu island, many are named Wayan. The first child that is, boy or girl. There are a few other options. The second child is Kadek, with, again, a few variations; the third is Nyoman, and the fourth, Ketut. The fifth? Wayan again.

After breakfast, Nobu takes a walk. "Where are you going?" the locals ask. *None of your business*, he used to think, but now he understands that it is a mere ritual here. *"Jalan Jalan,"* he answers. Taking a walk. He walks along the country road, where the offerings, pink flowers and flower-carved carrots, lie on woven rattan plates underneath bamboo trees.

Nobu gazes off to where the blue dawn turns gold, over the rice terrace, beside his bungalow. The morning sun drops itself equally into each pool of water, onto each stage of the rice terrace. Like hundreds of suns shining from within the earth. A white heron swoops down over the mirroring fields.

Smiling at Nobu, Wayan goes to his wife's bungalow with another tray. Emiko never eats fruit from the property, so Wayan must prepare a separate breakfast for her. The bungalows are designed as bachelor studios, each of them US$30 a month, so his company has rented two for the couple. A raspy voice comes over the hibiscus above Nobu's head. A man living in the bungalow next door has been on the phone for half an hour, speaking an unknown language. Dutch, Wayan once told him. And that he ran a kind of "amusement park" on this island.

Wayan comes back from Emiko's and says, "Mrs. Hamayama must be doing some chemical experiment." Nobu explains that it is a Japanese thing to wear a surgical mask all the time. His wife Emiko is always wearing a deep bucket hat and a hoody made of UV-proof synthetic cotton, sleeves stretching as far as the back of her hands, thumbs poking out from thumbholes. When she's outside, she shades her face with an umbrella. "Ah," Wayan says, "that's the secret of keeping that beautiful fair skin."

Well, Nobu thinks, that's a nice way to put it. He isn't very fond of his wife's ungainly outfit. He can't see her eyes; they are sunk in the shadow of the brim. Her family used to be Japanese nobility and this marriage is, for her, a downgrade. Nobu was a so-called *muko-yoshi*: to tie the knot, he had to be adopted into Emiko's family. Hamayama is her surname. She had been lured by the chance to be an expat's wife—though in Paris, not in Bali.

They seldom visit each other's bungalow. How free he feels, being alone in the bed again. How quickly he's forgotten the warmth of someone's skin, someone who once shared a bed with him. Emiko feels the same, perhaps. Once he visited her room while she was taking a shower. When she noticed him, she pulled the towel prudishly over her chest as she might to a stranger, and stalked off.

On the terrace, in front of his fruit platter, Nobu opens his day-planner. He has to get ready for the day's Skype meeting with his colleagues in Japan. He inclines his head over the planner. Sweat drops from his forehead and tints the page like a treasure map; it wrinkles. In this Indonesian languor he can't think of a single word to put down. His pencil drifts over the ruled page.

"Mr. Hamayama," Wayan says.

"Nobu," he chides her.

She blushes. "Nobu-san. Are you keeping a diary?"

Nobu doesn't know what to say. "Yes," he says, lying.

"Then write," she says, "you and I had some mango juice, here, today."

On Saturday, Nobu visits the Neka Art Museum. Through a shadowy grove and over the bridge he goes, and there it is, a peach-coloured house with an open tropical garden. The whole museum smells like some kind of wood. On the wall hangs a watercolour painting of a young Balinese girl. Her waist is wrapped in a long red ikat cloth, her upper half naked. The slight protrusions of her breasts are topped with tiny dark nipples like coffee beans. Nobu opens his *diary* and starts to sketch the painting. With his pencil he shades her skin and breasts. Wayan's face has swum into his mind. He draws a flower in the girl's hair.

In the evening, he watches the Kecak dance or Ramayana Monkey Chant in the town theatre. He tried to come with Emiko, but she wasn't interested. When the show is over, he waits for Kadek, Wayan's brother, to pick him up outside the theatre. *Kecak, kecak* the dancers chant in the lingering music.

Wayan shows up.

"So sorry, but Kadek couldn't make it," she says, and beckons him to the backseat of her Japanese scooter.

"You didn't have to come," Nobu says, "I could've made my way home."

"No, no. There are a lot of wild dogs on the way."

On the rear seat of the scooter, his arms wrapped around her waist, he smells the faint scent of her freshly washed hair, like a bouquet.

Hibiscus, bougainvillea? The dogs bark in the dark, their yellow crescent-shaped scratches of eyes drift in the blackness.

People from Nobu's company will be visiting the island next month. They are going to stay for five days. He has to make plans to entertain them. He leafs through his guidebook. Wayan walks by. He asks her advice.

"You could fly to Java, the neighbour island, for a day trip. They are Muslims, and yet they have the world's biggest Buddhist monument: Borobudur. I hear Japanese people love it. Your colleagues will like it too."

That sounds like a plan. She has a plate of some spiky, foul-smelling fruit in her hand. He winces at the stench. She reads his face and laughs.

That smells like … poop, thinks Nobu.

"It's called durian and it tastes divine! It's almost our national fruit, you must try it!"

"If I ate it, would you come with me to Java?"

She answers with a smile.

He holds his breath and tosses a tiny piece of the creamy flesh into his mouth. It tastes okay. Nutty, rich, slightly oniony.

"And?" she says.

"Not so bad," he says.

He opens his day planner. *Today, Wayan and I planned a trip, and ate some poop fruit.*

It was very sunny today. Wayan and I had a picnic. It was really nice.

Nobu writes, then scratches it out.

The meadow dappled with the sun and the clouds in green and grey. We had a picnic down by the river, Wayan and I, with grilled chicken sandwiches that she made. She tried to explain to me about the Ramayana dance I saw the other day. I asked …

He hears footsteps and looks up from his diary. Emiko is coming to his terrace. She plunks herself down on the bench beside him and opens her Japanese fashion magazine.

"There's a lizard in my room. So creepy."

"That must be a gecko." Geckos are cute, he thinks, but he doesn't say that to her. Instead, he says, "So we are taking Matsushita-san and Kawada-san to Borobudur next month."

She nods in silence.

"It's a UNESCO site, you wanna come?"

She keeps mum, flipping the pages of her magazine.

"I've found a nice restaurant to celebrate our wedding anniversary," he says, changing the topic. "It overlooks the rice terrace. Their chicken's great. Chicken's so great on this island; free range chickens, all of them!"

"I don't give a damn," she says. Emiko believes in raw foodism. "Besides, I doubt their hygiene standards."

"You can't say that." He tries to demur, though mildly.

Emiko closes her magazine with a slap and shoves it onto the table.

The party of four lands at Yogyakarta on Java. A van picks them up and they arrive at Borobudur. Among numbers of curvy stupas that look like round church bells, the biggest one on the top of the monument reminds Nobu of a breast; the breasts with coffee bean nipples he drew in the museum. Blasphemy, he thinks, and tries to shake off the thought.

In the afternoon they see a plume-like, carbon-grey cloud in the distance and in the next moment darkness has fallen over the sky. It starts to rain. The wind howls. They take refuge under a huge banyan tree in the middle of the square, their backs pushed by the gale. The branches of the trees flanking the square toss up and down, down and up, like necks of nervous horses. White, forked shoots of lightning are like lizard tongues, crisscrossing the black open sky, followed by a roar. Nobu looks around and realizes that Wayan isn't there.

"Where is she?" he asks his colleagues.

"She went to make a phone call to see if our flight is okay," one of them says.

"Alone?" Nobu says fretfully. The other two face each other and shrug. Nobu thinks of the blasphemous thought he had at the monument.

She returns soon after, drenched. Tiny raindrops drip from her long, curly eyelashes. "Our flight is cancelled," she says. "We have to stay on this island."

They rush through the downpour to a nearby street. Wayan finds a forlorn inn. The innkeeper balks, but in the end, he gives them rooms. After having vegetable soup in the dining hall, they retreat to their rooms.

Nobu is so excited he can't sleep. The rain is banging the windows and shingles, like those soybeans they throw at the beginning of the spring in Japan.

Fidgety, he goes to her room and knocks on the door. It swings open at once as if she was waiting right behind it. She smiles. She is bundled up in white bed linen, her hair still half wet. He takes off his half-wet shirt and dries her hair, tousling it; then kisses her.

The bombardment mutes the creak of the bed. Lightning flashes beyond the windows again and again, whitening her smoky-topaz skin under his coconut-oiled own; pearls of perspiration slip over her belly. He can't resist an impulse to add more sheen to it. He pulls himself out.

Next morning, he sees the blue sky through the dewy windows. A farmer with a cone-shaped hat is leading water buffaloes across the field, wading through the roiled soil.

The diary is open in front of him, but Nobu cannot write. *Today I was … I did … I.* Since the night in Java, he hasn't been able to complete a single sentence. Writer's block, he mutters to himself, and chuckles. Instead, he starts to draw. Wayan on a rung of the ladder, plucking bananas, her mango-shaped bottom quivering.

Nobu's trading company has just announced that it is going to end the "care-package service" to its expats. Up until now they have been receiving packages from home once a month, a box filled with Japanese goods. The company is sharply cutting expenses. Emiko freaks out. She needs her fashion magazines and face serum.

Two months later the company decides to withdraw from Indonesia, and Nobu's office is going to be closed. Emiko is happy to go back to Japan, but Nobu feels an odd twitch in his stomach. When she asks where in Tokyo they are going to live, he says, "I don't think I'm going back."

She raises her brows. "What did you just say?"

"I'm not going back."

She curls her lips, which makes her look like she's smiling. "Are you saying you are staying here?"

He nods.

"Quitting the company and staying on this primitive island?"

"Indonesia is said to be the next potential commercial hub. I could start my own business, perhaps."

"*Ooh*," she drawls. "And what about us? Are we splitting up?"

"If that's what you want."

Her cheeks swell and she bursts out laughing. "Are you out of mind?" she says, cupping his face with her hands. "Is that worth no longer being a Hamayama?"

He doesn't say anything.

"Suit yourself," she says. "Well, then. Get yourself a lawyer."

Three days later his wife leaves. She tells the taxi driver, whose language she has never learned, to go to the airport.

Nobu still doesn't know what to write. His pencil drifts tentatively over the blank page. Flipping it, he realizes that it is the last page. He muses for a while and starts to rip up the diary.

He doesn't know what to write so he knocks at her door. He knows Wayan is waiting, making a fruit platter, oiling her skin, smiling.

Gustafson and the Chinese

"What a powerful lunge!" The commentator says again. I look up. "Another point to Gustafson! Three minutes left, Gustafson with two-touch lead. The Chinese man doesn't look happy."

I squeeze the iron's handle. It stops on my husband's white dress shirt and soon there's a faint searing smell. Oh no, I can't burn his Hugo Boss.

I stare at the men on TV. Two fencers: one tall, the other short, both in white, step back and forth, forth and back, step, step, on a long, pale blue strip. "*Beauuutiful* counterattack there, Gustafson," the commentator says with a drawl. "Excellent shot! 14-11! But he's keeping his cool, the Chinese."

"*Zhong!*" I say. His name is Xianchao Zhong. I glance at the Chinese man's name on the subtitle. His masked face under the see-through visor. Self-control in his eyes. He doesn't even pinch his brows. Looks like my uncle, I think. My uncle who still lives in Hong Kong.

I was born there too, in Hong Kong. But I've been in Germany since I was 11. Why my parents chose this country, I don't know. Why not Britain, Canada, or the States? But Germany, that I haven't asked. My cousin lives in Vancouver. She says she likes it there.

I'm Cyndi. My real name is Vun-Moi, but who cares? Our names are too tough for them. So, we all pick dreamy, princessy names like Elizabeth, Angelina, Alexandra; blonde, long-legged names that we aren't. Cyndi, I took from Cyndi Lauper. She's a good one. Her quality must be *yang-gang*, bright and shiny. It's a good name. No frills, yet pretty.

"Gustafson—no, this time it's the Chinese! 14-12! That was a masterful *coup d'arrêt*."

What's that?

I look down at my husband's dress shirt. How odd. Since we launched our restaurant in this village, he's never really needed dress shirts. This is Schrollbach, population 300. Clouds dapple the hill. Pheasants sweep across the silver stream. Deer peek-a-boo from within the forest.

We rent this house from a village family. The ground floor is our restaurant; we live upstairs. The previous tenant ran a Hungarian restaurant and went bankrupt. He moved out, leaving all the kitchen facilities behind. I met the Hungarian owner once. Quantity matters, he said to me. Don't go too fancy.

That's true, in this bucolic land, quantity matters. We started the all-you-can-eat buffet. We are the first Chinese restaurant in the village. There are also German and Italian ones. That osteria isn't any good—but Americans come anyway.

Americans. Yes, our customers are mainly Americans.

The fencers dance on the strip. *Clink, clank*, the blades meet.

We are located near Ramstein, the largest U.S. Air Force base in Europe. When dollars are strong, the soldiers dine out every day.

That's fine. They are easygoing. They feast. They lavish tips on us. Some soldiers seem to have Asian or African backgrounds. We, Chinese, are nothing special to them.

But the locals, the villagers, are not like that. They stare at us. Do we look so different? Perhaps. Yet they can't tell me from other waitresses. Asian people all look the same, they say. Once, for a short period of time, I coloured my hair, blocked in red and yellow, just like Cyndi. Cyndi Lauper, someone started to call me. Then they started to recognize me. Then I became Cyndi.

Clink, clank, the blades clash, that's the *ding dong* of Tom's wok. Tom, my husband. He opens and slams the cupboard panels. Opens and slams.

"Where's the salt!" he yells.

"I'm ironing *your* shirts," I mumble.

He doesn't say anything. Being in this country longer than I, he still speaks German with a heavy accent. But we talk to each other in German anyway because he speaks Mandarin. He spends his last penny on his hobbies: body building, mah-jong gambling, cars. *Muscle Mustang*, they call him. He doesn't know, but I do.

Tom clumps towards me and stands in front of the ironing board, blocking out the TV. He sniffs. "It's expensive," he says, looking at the white Hugo Boss. "It's for tonight's meeting." He takes one look at me, and clumps away.

Lately he has so many meetings. And so many dress shirts.

Zhong the Chinese quickly steps forward, his left leg stretches behind, the tip of his sword touches the Swedish man's arm, it seems. "Gustafson's got a hit on his forearm," the commentator shouts. "Another point to the Chinese. Gustafson, show us your answer!"

I look at Zhong.

"Double touch," the commentator says.

On the wall of our restaurant hangs a huge photo panel of Hong Kong, the view from Victoria Peak. The highrises along the channel between Kowloon Peninsula and the island, lit up in the blue of the night, "the million dollar" view that you see on postcards. Every day before we open our restaurant, I look at it. I look at it for a long while. But what can we do? We're here for the euro. Euro is *teuro*, we used to say. *Teure*, expensive euro. Our sugar daddy euro.

But things are changing. A lot has happened since last year, 2010. "Fucking euro," Tom often says now. I don't know economics, but it must be good for Americans to have the weaker euro. They dine out even more frequently. But Tom doesn't understand. I want to say: Donate your brain to an organ bank if you aren't using it.

Should we go back to Hong Kong? I've been back twice. Before Reunification and after. In 1997, right before the return to China, it seemed deserted. But in 2005, the people were back and tourists were back, and I loved the liveliness of it. I can speak Cantonese with no accent. They didn't realize that I'd left there long ago, and so treated me as one of them.

But I don't belong to Hong Kong either.

When I walked through the bird market, I thought of bird flu. I didn't feel like eating at food stands on Tung-Choi Street like everyone else.

But I loved Stanley, the other side of Hong Kong Island, where all the expats lived. The air-conditioned double-deckers drove over the hill, threaded through the woods, and there you were, in Stanley, where numerous white yachts heedlessly floated on the cobalt ocean. In Murray House, the beautiful colonial building, you could have tapas, pizza, or German beer, overlooking the sea.

In the spacious supermarket in Stanley, in the ice-cold air conditioning, you see everything the Westerners need: Ribena for the Brits, Hershey's for the Americans, and Dr. Oetker for the Germans. Canadian maple syrup. How I felt at home.

And then I saw myself. My own silhouette reflected on the glass window of the freezer shelf: a short, dark-haired Asian woman. I was like a dog that had grown up among humans, never realizing that it wasn't one of them. An Asian duck that thought it was a swan.

Clink, clank the blades. No, it's the telephone ringing.

I walk to the kitchenette through the heavy smell of ripe peaches. "Nine Dragons Restaurant," I say.

"Vun-Moi, it's me," my sister says at the other end. "I have good news. We've got the permit!"

"That's wonderful!" We've been talking to the Ramstein management and now we can open a Nine Dragons outlet in the Commissary inside the base.

"We're going to get that tiny space next to the Starbucks," Gyuk-Kiao says.

Tom starts to slam the cupboard panels again. I glare at him.

"Are you still there?" Gyuk-Kiao asks. "You know, perhaps we'll be allowed to shop their American stuff in the mall. It'd be so nice. Oh. They have those beautiful short ribs, American beef. Beef in this country sucks, you know that—"

I look at the TV. The score is now even: 14-14. Shoot, I missed the equalizer. "Double touch again," the commentator says.

"We're going to have a meeting on Friday, Vun-Moi. You're in, aren't you?"

Zhong is stamping his front foot. Suddenly he dashes forward and corners Gustafson. At the edge of the strip Zhong half swoops down and twists his upper body, and his blade surprises Gustafson's lower leg.

The commentator yells. "This is it! Fifteen for the Chinese! The Chinese won!" Applause, applause. "Great action there." The commentator's clever chat goes on. "It's like baseball ... when a pitcher wants to change a batter's eye level ..."

"And Vun-Moi, my little sister, don't eat too much baked stuff. It's not good for you. You have too much *heat* in you. Have some winter melon soup."

There's still applause. I turn off the TV and Zhong's masked face.

Suddenly the dull roar of jet engines comes into the room through the crack of the tilted window sash. I look up at an inky silhouette against the darkening sky, forging its way toward Landstuhl.

So, that is the aircraft with lucky soldiers aboard, the soldiers from Iraq, to be treated at the hospital in Landstuhl.

Looking at the shadow I think about wounded soldiers who are left behind on the battlefield, their unknown faces, as faceless as I am here.

I stand in front of our tiny garden. A cluster of tomatoes sags among the arugula bush, grown unappetizingly high. Eggplants are lustrous in the blazing sun, metallic violet. I look at a giant, football-like green fruit. Who started to call them *winter* melons? I pull its tendril and tug it toward me. Wow, it's heavy. It crushes the oregano leaves, and their spicy aroma wafts up into the air. I cut the tendril, heave the fruit and put it aside.

You have too much *heat* in you, my sister said. Cool down.

Cool down what?

I'm 40. I'm physically here but hardly living. That's what I realized upon turning 40. That you can't be anything that you aren't.

I was born into the bustle of the city and that's where I belong. The house, the garden where I can grow veggies, the greenness, the soil, the things that used to bring me trifling joy, don't mean anything anymore. I miss apartments. Highrises. Crowds on the streets. Voices. Conversations.

Love.

My love is strong. To love is an ability, and I am talented. Yet I'm tethered to this loveless unit, in this malnutrition, on the verge of starvation. What is the heat to be cooled down?

I heave the winter melon and gaze into the street. A passerby—a villager—nods at me. I leave the courtyard and go around the house to the front door. J.J. doesn't seem to be in the kitchen. J.J., a Chinese cook whom Tom has recruited from the Peninsula Hotel in Hong Kong, or so he says, doesn't like to have me around the kitchen. I stealthily enter and place the melon on the cutting board. *Thud.* I chop it in half, its gelatinous seeds splatter. I scoop the seeds out, and then scoop the white flesh out. The flesh, which is supposed to make me a cooler person.

I shove two stew pots onto the cooktop and begin to cook them. Over the boiling water I hear a car being parked outside. Shit, is J.J. back? I peek out of the window. No, it's not him.

There stands a short, middle-aged man, a bit stout, yet not fat. His hair is a curly auburn, his high cheeks rosy; a square-shaped pince-nez sits on his high nose. Bolt upright, standing like a statue.

Beautiful, I think. Is it okay to call a man beautiful?

I go outside. He's staring at the menu while standing in front of our restaurant. "Hi," I say in English. By hunch I know he's not German. But he doesn't look like a soldier either. What is he doing in this village then?

"Hi," he says, his voice deep. "Do you have this buffet on Saturdays too? Looks really nice."

"Yes, we do. But it's the afternoon break right now. We open again at 6 for dinner."

"Oh, I see." He looks at his watch. "I'll come back later, then."

Later that night the man shows up. I lead him to a table in the corner. It's 9 p.m. and people have started to leave. By the time I bring him a postprandial plum wine, it is just the two of us in the restaurant. We begin to chat.

His name is Nico. He's American. He's a military theorist at the base. His wife is a physician, active-duty Major in the Army, he says, and serving in Iraq. He lives in Kaiserslautern, where "the slope starts to ascend toward the university."

"Maybe we can go for a coffee sometime," he says. He leaves his business card together with his payment.

How lovely that he asks me for a coffee. The villagers don't even think I drink coffee.

In a café in Kaiserslautern, I sit across from him over coffee. I take a sip of my macchiato. He is looking at me, smiling.

"So, you are from Chicago," I say.

"Yes."

"And you are Greek-American."

"Yes."

"What does that mean?"

He chuckles. "That means I am Greek and I am American. Like you, Chinese-German."

"I'm not German," I say crossly. But I'm not Chinese either, I guess. What am I?

He's still watching me drinking my macchiato. I delve into the milk foam with a wooden stick and lick it.

"I've never seen a girl who enjoys coffee so seriously," he says.

Girl, he calls me.

In the bathtub I stare at my toes. The dark brown nail lacquer, which I put on a few months ago, barely remains at the tips of my naked, vanilla toenails. Looks like caramel pudding, I think, looking at the dark colour on top. The hair on my shins sways in the water like seaweed. So unprepared. So not ready to be exposed to someone else's eyes. I turn the handle on the drain. As the water descends, its surface slowly, gently, brushes my privates. I can't move. I bend slightly backward, freeze two minutes and let the water lick down my slit.

I sit up and grab Tom's razor.

It's 3 o'clock in the afternoon. I'm going to sneak into the restaurant kitchen. It's the afternoon break again. Hopefully J.J. isn't there. I am going to heat up the frozen winter melon soup cubes I made the other day. I hear a car being parked outside. I stick my head out of the window.

"Hey Cyndi," one of our American customers says. "Good to see you. Did you have a good time in Frankfurt?"

Frankfurt?

"I saw you and *Muscle*——." The man grins. "Er——I mean Tom, at Haubtwache. And yeah, J.J. too. Hey, you looked stunning in that little black dress——"

Ah, classic.

So, that's why he needs so many dress shirts lately. Classic. Am I hurt? Hell no. Then why am I upset? I think of the freedom he has. WHERE IS MINE?

I dump the soup in the sink. Scuttling up the stairs from the kitchen, I think of Nico. In the den, I fumble in the drawers and grab some cash. I see my ID card—and my passport—and grab them too. My silver bracelet is on the coffee table; I grab it as well. I throw anything that comes into my view into a gym bag. My wallet, my phone. A tube of lipstick.

Before I realize it, I am in Kaiserslautern. How I have come here, I don't remember. Did I turn off the heat on the cooktop? I don't care.

Bus after bus, and I'm at where "the slope starts to ascend to the university." It has started to rain and is dark.

I have prowled around for half an hour when I find a dark blue Ford Focus with a U.S. military license plate parked in front of a house. Beside it, a red Mini. I look up at the window of the house.

The light is on. I gaze up at it for a while, completely soaked, looking for his face. There he is, the profile with eyeglasses, noble as a Greek statue.

Beside him is a shapely woman, smiling. Her blond hair in a Rachel cut, smart as a model in the ads of American apparel companies.

I'm standing at the bus stop. In the rain, away from the covered waiting area, my black gym bag in my hand. People stare at me.

In 10 minutes, the bus comes that will take me home.

On the other side of the street is another bus stop. Where do those buses go? In the other direction, away from home. I think of home. I have nothing to lose. I think of Frankfurt, the nearest big city. And of the airport.

America.

Chicago. Where that beautiful man comes from. I think of the skyscrapers at the lake.

Two headlights approach, on my side, and a car *swooshes* over the wet asphalt and passes in front of me. I shade myself with a hand against the splash.

And it's gone.

On the other side, I see another set of headlights.

April Fools' Day

When I come downstairs, Mommy's already dressed. You know why this is funny? Because I almost always get up before she does. I get up at quarter to eight because my school starts at half past eight. I go to Oakville Public School and I'm in the second grade.

Mommy is in a suit the colour of whole grain bread she only wears when she has job interviews. I last saw her in this outfit before Christmas.

Good morning, Mommy, I say, and try to kiss her lips, but Mommy tilts her head and I end up kissing her cheek. During the day I always kiss Mommy's lips, only Mommy can kiss my lips, but in the morning, she always tilts her head. Onion breath, she says, but it's not onion. It's like fish out of a muddy pond. It's just coffee, I say to her anyway. You look nice. Did you buy Olay?

Not yet, she says.

You should, I say. It will make you beautiful. I saw it on TV. I promise to buy her an Olay cream, and that Jell-O thing that removes hairs from shins.

Breakfast? she asks. I can make some pancakes for you.

But it's not Sunday, I say. Mommy and I have breakfast together only on Sundays. During the week I eat a bowl of Rice Krispies while she's still in bed. Sometimes I feed Sarah too. Sarah is my sister. She's 4. But I have to be careful because she has a nut allergy. I do the dishes too. I mean I put the bowls and plates in the dishwasher. Daddy usually puts the bowl he uses in the sink and leaves home, at what time I don't know, so I put it in the dishwasher too.

Every morning there are empty bottles on the dishwasher. One wine bottle and some beer bottles. Mommy loves red wine and drinks one bottle every night. Sometimes she drinks yellow wine too.

But today, the bottles are gone. I smooth the surface of the machine. The butter sizzles on the cooktop. Ma, the butter, I say. But she doesn't seem to hear. She's at the table, looking at the air.

Not many things are on the countertop either. It's made of nice dark stone, smooth and shiny. Granite, Mommy once said proudly. I find a wrinkled yellow balloon on it.

That's the balloon I saw at school some days ago. I was inside waiting for the bell ring. Through the glass pane on the door, I looked outside and saw Jason's Mommy and Alisha's Mommy there for the pickup. My Mommy was there too. She was playing with Sarah, with the yellow balloon. I heard no sound. It was like a TV with the sound off, watching Mommy and Sarah. They seemed so happy. So happy in the world without me.

Mommy still doesn't move, so I pour the pancake batter into the frying pan. It sizzles. Do we still have maple syrup?

Mommy stands up and comes over to me. She crouches down and now her eyes are below mine. I like it when she does that. I like it when Mommy's eyes are close to mine.

Look, she says. I have to go somewhere when Sarah wakes up.

Where? I say.

Kind of a far place, she says.

Where? I ask again. Will you get some Timbits for me on the way back?

Maybe, she says. You'll listen to your Daddy, will you?

But Daddy is never home.

I'll get Ms. Davis in the afternoon. She's going to do the pickup.

Are you going downtown? I ask.

I'll come back as soon as possible and pick you up, okay?

Will you get some Timbits on the way back? I ask again.

Yes. And you'll be a good boy till I come back, will ya?

I nod. There's the burnt smell of flour but she doesn't rise. I look into the hall and there stands a suitcase. It's not the grey one she used to have. It's a red one and I've never seen it before. It has a nametag, also red. Maybe she's taking a flight; she said she'd be going far away.

Will you come back by Thursday? It's Dance-a-thon and I'll be dancing a Hindu dance.

I'll see what I can do, she says. Maybe I can get Ms. Davis for this too. I'll try.

Try means it won't happen. I know it but I don't say it to her.

But maybe she doesn't mean it. She's not going far away or calling Ms. Davis or even *trying*. She'll be home with Timbits tonight; onion breath and empty bottles tomorrow. Just today may be different. Because it is April Fools' Day.

Soda Pop Candy

Yuki's house stood in the middle of a slope. Ten identical units of houses lined alongside the slope on the left side. These were owned by a Japanese broadcasting corporation and rented out to its employees. The positions of the houses represented their male occupants' positions in the company. Yuki's was the third from the bottom.

On the top of the hill stood the Matsudas where Yuki's friends, Sakura and Goro, lived. The right side of the slope was a farm. Beyond the carrot field loomed a stable where cows mooed in the mornings, during the days and sometimes at nights. This bucolic neighbourhood was part of Yokohama. It was the early 1970s.

On the other side of the hill, at the bottom of the slope, was a small shopping mall. Yuki and her mother went there every day. The floors were unpaved, the sheet-metaled roof corrugated, the naked bulbs dropped dim circles on the earthy ground. The lights were dim because in some far, far-away countries, rich people decided to raise the oil prices. At the drugstore, Yuki's mother complained about the toilet paper prices.

On Fridays the butcher shop sold chicken drumsticks and they were Yuki's favourite. She called them Friday Meat. Wednesday Meat was whale meat, which people like the Matsudas would never have touched, but Yuki's mother bought it sometimes. It tasted a little like beef but was much cheaper.

The Matsudas soon moved to the United Kingdom. Mr. Matsuda was supposed to work at the BBC for three years as part of their exchange programs. Sakura and Goro were gone, and Yuki had no other friends in the area. A few months later she received a small package from the United Kingdom. It was a bag of gumdrops. Yuki had never seen black gumdrops. *Liquorice* was written on the packaging.

White and mauve moss phloxes were in bloom. Strawberries were inches above the soil, creeping on the ground beside them. Yuki crouched down, picked a ripe strawberry and tossed it into her mouth. She had never had such a sweet strawberry. Then she heard a merry voice and a *thwack*. She stood up. The voice came from over the concrete wall that faced her next-door neighbour's backyard, on the lower side of the hill. She went up to the wall and, on tiptoe, looked down into their backyard, her hands squeezing the top of the wall. Two girls, aged perhaps six and eight, a little older than Yuki herself, were playing together with jump ropes. The older girl seemed to have noticed Yuki from the corner of her eye, but she didn't say anything. They had just moved in a few weeks before. The sisters hadn't made any friends yet, but they had each other.

Yuki had a sandbox, a swing, and a small trampoline but she didn't have a sibling. The swing was a two-seater face-to-face type, and when she was on it, her side sank and creaked. She needed company. She named her imaginary friend Akira. "Do you like the swing?" she asked him, the swing still sinking and creaking on the same side.

Since Sakura and Goro moved away, Yuki had to spend endless hours with adults, especially with her mother. Yuki's father was seldom home. *Japan is striving, so is your father; you must understand*, her mother would say.

Yuki remembered two nights with her father. One night he brought her a wooden, antique transistor radio. In Japan, shortwave listening was a popular hobby in the seventies. He tuned into the BBC, and they heard Mr. Matsuda read the news among the sandy noise.

That was the good night.

Yuki's family slept in the same cramped tatami room, in "kawa no ji," the shape of a kanji character that meant "river." The ideal form for a family to sleep, in three vertical lines, the parents outside and the child inside. One night Yuki woke up in the middle of the night, her father's *sake*-breath and clammy hand were unnecessarily close to her.

That was the bad night.

"We are going on a field trip to The Viper Valley on Thursday," Yuki's kindergarten teacher, Ms. Katada said. Yuki couldn't have been more excited. The Viper Valley. Japanese pit vipers were said to have magical powers. Maybe if she found one, it could listen to one or two of her wishes.

In the valley she strolled among mock strawberries looking for a viper. Now she stood alone by the brook. She had lagged behind the group and began to feel scared. Then a boy from her class showed up from behind a bush. She felt relieved. Kunio was a big boy, a son of a popular sushi restaurant owner in town. He could take her back to the group.

A bunch of other boys in her class appeared, following Kunio. They formed a circle and surrounded Yuki.

"What are you doing here all by yourself?" Kunio asked.

"I was looking for a viper," she answered.

The on-looking boys chuckled. She looked at Kunio, expecting him to say a kind, soothing word. He grinned but didn't say anything. His hair was cut short, almost bald. The top of his head, where his hair was, seemed slightly green and looked like a young, poisonous potato with a green, map-like stain. As Kunio's grin widened, the boys started to laugh. Yuki didn't know what to do; she didn't have siblings who laughed at her.

Kunio then turned around and eyed his boys. The boys stepped forward and made the circle smaller. Yuki stood in the centre of it.

"Take off your skirt, and take off your underwear," Kunio said.

She understood clearly what she had been ordered to do, but she was not used to talking back or asking *what*. I think I'm in trouble, she said to herself. Akira, she called her imaginary friend in her mind. Akira, I think you should come here right now to save me. Akira. Akira?

Akira didn't respond and Kunio repeated his command. She took off her skirt and underwear. Kunio and the boys burst out laughing. Yuki looked down on the grassy ground, ashamed, not knowing what she was supposed to say.

"Nice butt," Kunio said. The boys laughed harder.

Out of the corner of her eye, Yuki noticed something bob. She turned her eyes to the top of the hill. A girl from her class was looking down into the valley at them. When she ran off, Yuki felt relieved. The girl would get Ms. Katada and everything would be fine. Yuki threw a hopeful gaze in the direction in which the girl disappeared.

Back at kindergarten, Ms. Katada told Yuki to remain in the classroom. The other children had already been picked up and she was alone in the room with her teacher.

"Rika-chan told me that you made water in the valley. Did you?" Ms. Katada asked, but actually she was telling.

Yuki didn't say anything. She looked down.

"Yes?" Ms. Katada said. "You know you were not supposed to pee like that, surely you know that."

Yuki still looking down, remained silent. A tear dropped on her cheek.

"I'll have to tell your mother about this," the teacher said and called in Yuki's mother, who had been waiting outside.

That's good, mama is coming now, Yuki thought. Mama knows that I cry only when I'm angry.

Her mother came in and escorted Yuki out, nudging her back, apologizing to the teacher again and again. All the way home, her mother kept asking her why she had done that, saying how disappointed she was.

Yuki didn't say anything.

Yuki was at the candy shop in the mall. Her mother was across the alley, looking into the butcher's glass showcase. The owner of the candy shop was an old man, sitting at the checkout, his face sunk behind a newspaper. There were shelves, standing in a dead angle from him. Yuki hid herself behind them. Displayed on the shelves were small candy boxes that were miniature look-alike plastic cans of soda pop: Coke, Fanta, Sprite. In those cans were white fizzing tablets with a given flavour.

Yuki stared at them for a long while. She was thinking of Akira. She hadn't talked to him since the field trip. Perhaps they'd need something to break the long silence. Maybe Akira would like some soda pop candy. She peeked through the shelves. Her mother was still chatting with the butcher, the old man still reading his newspaper.

One container of soda pop candy was 20 yen. She groped in her pockets and found 10 yen. She looked out again. The old man didn't seem to notice she was there. Yuki picked up a can of Fanta Orange. She broke the seal and twisted the lid. Tiny white pills were in there. The artificial orange smell wafted. Maybe just half of this, she thought. Just half. She opened her left palm and gingerly poured half the can into it. Making a fist, she slunk away from the candy shop. The old man hadn't taken his eyes off the paper.

Yuki had a last look at her mother's back at the meat shop. Right then her mother turned around and their eyes met. "Yuki," her mother called, waving, stepping forward. "I've got some Friday Meat for you!"

Upon hearing that, Yuki scampered out of her way, and out of the shopping mall.

She ran up the slope, clenching her fist. Her hand became moist, and the candy started to melt. And she ran. Uphill and downhill. Ran and ran, passing in front of the former Matsuda house, passing the farm. The cows mooed.

She was approaching her house, the third unit from the bottom of the hill, when she fell. She should have listened to her mother; her mother always told her never to run downhill. Yuki's body slid down a meter or two, down the slant of the cobbles. She felt the burn on her right knee, her left arm catapulting toward the front.

Her left palm opened. The tiny white pills tumbled out and rolled down the slope, farther, and farther away.

White Asparagus Soup

"I'm going out," her now-officially-ex yells from downstairs.

She yells back from her bedroom: "I'm leaving in about an hour. Will you be back by then?"

"I don't know," he says. "Maybe."

She hears the front door close.

She goes downstairs. His shoes are nowhere to be seen. A space on the coatrack. In the kitchen, on the island is a half-dried out bouquet of red roses in a terracotta vase. A russet petal falls and makes a rustle. A stainless-steel pot is left on the stove.

"Ah," she says. She forgot about that. Last night they made some broth from white asparagus scraps.

Last night they ate some white asparagus, *Spargel*, bought in a German store in Greenville. It was the end of the season and he wanted to have the dish one last time before he moved to China for work. She peeled the thick white cobs at the sink. Fibrous peels heaped up on a sheet of newspaper.

While the asparagus boiled, she made some Hollandaise sauce, as usual. "Dinner is ready," she called. He was on the phone. She overheard him saying: "... at my wife's place ... call you back ..."

My wife. She half smiled.

He came into the kitchen. The ribbons of asparagus peel were still on the paper, curled up and browned like huge pencil shavings.

"It's kind of sad to dump them, isn't it?" he said, looking sideways at the peelings. "Why don't we make some asparagus soup tomorrow?"

"From scratch?" she said. "I've never done that before."

They liked white asparagus soup but always made it from soup mixes. Why not? Those mixes tasted good enough.

He picked up his phone and called his mother.

"Just boil the peelings, make some béchamel sauce, and dilute it with the broth." Rephrasing what his mother had told him in German, he hung up. He scooped up the peelings with his hands and put them into a pot, then pressed the top down. "I'm sure you can make whatever béchamel sauce is."

She was sure she could make the white sauce. She loved cooking and he knew that.

He had been her husband for five years. When they were summoned to court a few weeks before, she had found out that he had been staying at an Airbnb after breaking up with his girlfriend, not having been able to get a place on a short-term lease. "Come to my place, then," she had said to him outside courtroom 207.

That raised many eyebrows. "Don't you have any pride?" her girlfriends said. She didn't care what they said; it wasn't they who were going through a divorce. A couple of them weren't even married. "I hear something!" others said in a knowing voice, their eyes wide with inquisitiveness, their elbows nudging her waist, as if they were teasing her about a juicy new story, as if they believed the couple would be getting back together. Did they seriously think they'd spent thousands of dollars on lawyers to reunite like this? She wanted to laugh.

She lifts the lid and puts it aside. The peelings have shrunk and sunk to the bottom of the water. Spooning the broth toward her mouth, she catches a whiff of the grassy smell.

She takes a saucepan from a drawer and throws a chunk of butter into it. When it melts, she adds flour. Soon wafts a cookie-like smell of the burnt butter, and the yellowish paste starts to bubble. She pours some hot milk into the pan. With a whisk she stirs it hard. Bringing it to boil again, she continues to stir, making a metallic *swish*. Finally, the mixture becomes smooth, thick and glossy. She looks at the clock. It has been half an hour since he left, and she too has to leave soon.

She doesn't know where he is. She doesn't know why he needs to do it when he has to leave soon for the airport to catch his flight for China. It's not worth the hassle. But it's none of her business anymore, she knows that, whatever he does. Nothing has to make a single piece of sense to her any longer. He is just someone who is staying in her guest room, for a split second, to share their last moment.

Rainwater has started tapping on the windows. Just like that day, over two years ago, when the tearing noise of the telephone ripped the silence, among the tapping of rainwater, while she was standing in the kitchen.

"I saw him," a friend said over the phone. She said she'd seen him on a Friday night in a fancy Italian restaurant. With a slightly older brunette; a sophisticated kind of woman. "You know," the friend continued in a lowered voice, and paused on a word as if she'd been about to announce a gruesome fact. "He wasn't wearing his ring."

Maybe this friend didn't know: she hadn't been wearing her ring either since her last pregnancy. Her fingers had swollen like parsnips and she couldn't wear the ring anymore; he also took off his ring to show empathy. Or perhaps he was just not a ring person.

It was a miscarriage.

They were still young enough for a second try. But the taste of loss left in their mouths was so bitter that they thought they'd need some time off.

It was an unplanned pregnancy. Because it was unplanned, people acted as though it didn't matter that they lost the child. They said they should try again. They said it should "cure" soon, as if grief was a disease or something.

They hadn't worn their rings since then.

That night when she asked her husband about the other woman, he said *I'm sorry*. He moved out the next day.

He was sorry. But perhaps it was she who should have been sorry. It was, after all, she who had kept refusing him, chased him away and deserted their bed.

After adding a pinch of salt and white pepper to the béchamel sauce, she grinds nutmeg over the pan. The sauce is ready. Now it's time to make the soup. She adds a ladle of the asparagus broth into the white mixture and keeps stirring it, allowing no lumps to form while coddling.

Is this enough? she wonders. For the soup? No need to add extra vegetable broth or chicken stock? How much salt? The asparagus broth isn't much; does it have enough umami? The white sauce looks perfect, but it seems too thick to be diluted with so little broth. Her former mother-in-law's face has swum into her mind, but she doesn't feel like asking her. They have already been estranged.

Google? Yes, Google.

She sets the white sauce aside, takes out another skillet and starts over to make a new sauce, adding much less flour this time. *Whip, whip, whip.* Gradually she begins to feel rejuvenated. It's been a while since she last cooked for someone. For someone, whether he eats it or not.

But why am I taking this so seriously? she says to herself. It's just soup. I'd rather make lasagne—his favourite—than this. Still, she wants to make a perfect whatever, for this will probably be the last time she cooks for him. It's just soup, nothing fancy, and what she has now is the chance to make this soup. White asparagus soup.

Six years ago, she met him at a friend's birthday party. He wasn't really her type and they had little in common. But he was nice and ordinary. She'd wanted to marry a man who was nice and ordinary. She was 29, ordinary, and tired of searching. He was 31 and wanted to marry her. Was she to blame for saying *yes*?

During the first years, they tried to spend as much time together as possible, he reading her books, she playing his games. Soon he began model railroading, she mandala colouring, in their own spaces.

Wednesday afternoons were her half-days off, but those were the evenings her husband would go to a pub after playing soccer with his work crew, so she spent long half days on her own.

One Wednesday evening in February, she attended a book launch at an independent bookstore. She knew the author, but she couldn't wade through the people to get to the front. Instead, she grabbed a cookie and found a spot at the back of the crowd. Standing next to her was a man she'd never met. Well into his forties, tall and sculpted, his face was shiny and smooth for his age, oddly contrasting with his all-grey, wavy hair. He seemed to be part Asian. When their eyes met, he smiled. "What a great turnout, huh? Good for her."

"It sure is," she said. "I know her from my yoga class. I just wanted to say hello, but—it doesn't look like I have a chance."

"Really? She's my former co-worker. I used to be a librarian," he said.

The author was still surrounded by the crowd. Outside the window she saw flurries. She felt cold, but there were only soft drinks in the room. She donned her white knit cap and pulled it over her ears.

"It's freezing in here," the man said. "Would you care for a glass of mulled wine? Rodney's makes good stuff."

They sneaked out and went to the café across the street.

It was 8, but Rodney's Café was lively. When they entered, the toasty air of the room pricked her frozen cheeks. The spicy aroma of mulled wine—cinnamon, clove, orange—stung her nose.

"So, you were a librarian," she said, her hands around the warm cup, her nose slightly rosy. "I don't have many to exchange, but—how about a book swap for March?" She sipped her warm red wine. "The winter's been too long. I've already read all my books! I feel like reading something that I would otherwise never come across. Something new, something provoking, something exotic."

They decided to meet up again at Rodney's.

On the second Wednesday after the book launch, they met again for the first book swap. It was the middle of March, and the sun was regaining its strength. On the way to the café, she tripped over the muddy, melting pile of snow at the curb while looking up at the young leaves of poplars flanking the promenade, shining silvery in the sunlight. It was like an early sample of spring. When she opened the door to the café, the warm air and sweet, nutty smell brushed her cold cheeks.

The man handed her a novel, *Silence*, written by the Japanese writer Shusaku Endo.

"Ah, I know this," she said. "The film."

"Did you see it?" he asked.

"Actually no," she said, running her fingers over the cover.

When she returned home, her husband was there. He was separating papers and flyers, carefully examining whether there were any coupons, and then tossing them into the recycle bin.

"Hi, you're here," she said, laying Endo's book on the kitchen island. He gave a stolid glance at it and went back separating the papers. She noticed, on the back of the paper, an announcement of a forthcoming blues festival in town.

"Hey, the blues festival is coming," she said.

"Oh yeah?" he said. "I don't like the blues."

"How was it?" the man asked, at Rodney's.

"Well," she said, leafing through Endo's book and stopping on a page where a bookmark was sticking out. She laid her eyes on the lines: Sin, he reflected, is not what it is usually thought to be; it is not to steal and tell lies. *Sin is for one man to walk brutally over the life of another and to be quite oblivious of the wounds he has left behind.*

She said, "I found these lines so profound."

She thought about her angel baby—baby boy, she would always imagine. Her body still tried to recall the empty memory. He'd walked over her life and left a wound behind. But was that sinful? No, the sin wasn't his.

"Why did you pick it for me?" she asked.

"You wanted exotic," he said, teasingly.

As if he had known she would like another Japanese writer, he had Yukio Mishima for this meeting.

"Aside from his political view, Mishima is worth reading," the man said, his voice clear and solemn like that of a professor. If it hadn't been Kawabata, it had been Mishima who was to receive the Nobel Literature Prize, he added, handing her the next book: *Confession of a Mask.*

So, Mishima was a bisexual; she'd learned that from the book. It wasn't from the famous *The Sea of Fertility* series but an independent title. A memoir disguised as fiction. His confession. A story of a young man who struggled to fit, or not fit, into an androcentric society during wartime. In the story, he picked some books for a girl whom he desperately tried to love but didn't mention the titles. She wondered what they were.

And she wondered what the man would pick for her next.

How nice. Someone finally understands the things you love! Closing her eyes, she recalled his deep voice. She opened the window to get some fresh air. Birds warbled. From the walk-in closet she chose a brand-new, light-coloured dress, and went off to the fourth meeting. As if he had known what she wanted, again he gave her another Mishima: *After the Banquet*.

On the way to the fifth meeting with the book man, she dropped by a nail salon she had recently discovered. The manicurists didn't scrape your nails too vigorously as some others did when applying gel polish.

"What colour?" the woman asked.

"Red," she said.

"*After the Banquet* was amazing!" This book was an easier read for her than the first two. Here, Mishima, unlike his confession, was perfectly invisible as the narrator. She'd delved into it. The story was based on the real life of a quixotic former foreign minister and his newlywed wife, who wasn't high-born like her husband. "It's amazing how well he knows women—how she gets attracted by a much older, intelligent man, how she, this portly lady relaxes in a half-open kimono undergarment, ungainly yet sultry, how a woman can be so natural and carefree in front of a man who she doesn't care about, and how she becomes rigid in front of her lover! How does he know!" she said, her cheeks rosy with excitement.

"Maybe he grew up with lots of sisters or something, I don't know," he said, and smiled. It was a beautiful smile. "You too?"

"Sisters? Oh, I—."

"No," said the man. "You too?"

She didn't understand what he meant. His eyes behind the glasses were penetrating.

"A woman doesn't care how she looks in front of a man to whom she's not attracted? Is that true?"

She felt her cheeks blush. Flashing him a quick smile, she sipped her coffee, and lowered her gaze to the subtle green of her slice of avocado cream cheesecake. She thought he could see through her little black dress.

"I think I know what *this* woman is thinking," he said, layering his large hand over her red-nailed hand on the table.

Tripping down the street afterward in the late afternoon, she chewed over what he had said. Warm rays emanated through a window. She'd always loved this time of the day. Lights came on in houses down the street, but too early for the residents to realize they should pull their curtains. Invisible lives during the day popped up in warm yellow frames of light, like scenes from puppet shows. She couldn't help turning to each window. The characters in the shows were so heedless they didn't realize they were being watched. In one window, a young couple was in the kitchen. Two cheap replicas of Monet hung on the wall. Under a kitschy plastic lampshade, the couple laughed, fixing a salad together. They might be talking about their day. She tried to recall when she had last asked her husband how his day had been. In another window she saw a family with a toddler. She reflected on *After the Banquet*, its protagonist. Her intolerance with stillness, her craving for motion, changes, life. LIFE.

In her neighbour's shrubs she noticed some white blossoms blooming, poking through the thin layer of snow. She stopped to smell them. Spring was coming. She looked up. There was a white spool of cloud in the mauve sky, busy untangling itself. She wanted to see how it dissolved. She stared at it but couldn't see it shrinking. She held her eyes open without blinking. The changes weren't visible, but the cloud kept dwindling. In plain sight, the cloud dissipated, leaving no vestige of what had been.

It was the last Wednesday of April. The married couple ran into each other in their driveway.

"You dressed up," he said, looking at her.

"I'm going to have a late night," she said.

He didn't say anything.

She wanted to say: I'm falling for another man. She almost did. Not to her friends, not to her mother, it was to him she really wanted to tell the truth. Their marriage had long been over, and this man had given her a chance to re-live. She wanted him to know that. She wanted to say *I'm sorry and I couldn't help it*. But she knew she shouldn't. He wouldn't be able to deal with it. Instead of saying so, she emptied their bedroom the next day and started sleeping in the guest room.

The soup seems perfect now. She writes a message on a piece of green sticky note and puts it on the pot lid: I'm going out to lunch with a friend. You can have the soup.

Maybe he will have the soup.

Maybe not.

When she comes back home, no one is there. It's 2:40. He must have already gone. She goes into the kitchen. His laptop, which was left open on the dining table this morning, isn't there. The sticky note has fallen from the pot lid onto the cooktop. She lifts the lid. The soup, it seems, is untouched.

Disappointed? Maybe a little. It was he who suggested they make soup. But nothing upsets her anymore. She looks back on their lives together. His goofy expressions—his chin sagging slackly and eyes half open—while he brushed his teeth; a pant hem tucked in a white, schoolboy sock; Tupperware lids that weren't stored together with containers; short pencils he filched from IKEA every time he went there. What once drove her crazy now makes her smile.

She recalls Endo's line in *Silence: sin is for one man to walk brutally over the life of another and to be quite oblivious of the wounds he has left behind.*

Perhaps she shouldn't have married him. He could've been much happier with another woman. It is she who walked brutally over his life. She's glad it is he who has walked away. She hopes he is oblivious of the wounds he has left behind.

She looks at the red roses on the kitchen island. The petals are gathering pigments at their edges. She always likes flowers best when they are about to end their lives. The colour becomes intense. The moment they look most alive.

She heats the soup and pours it into a bowl. She brings a spoonful to her lips. Tears well from her eyes. It's not savory enough but tastes all right. All right together with the bitter-sweetness deep in her throat.

The Ovulation Blues

On the second floor of an Asia-fusion restaurant on Bahnhofstrasse, Maya was mentally correcting misspellings on the blackboard when Allison texted her: *Where are you?*

Upstairs.

The jerks said we don't have a spot without a reservation.

I've got a spot. I told them I was waiting for a friend.

What a jerk. I'm walking back then.

While she waited for Allison, her long-time Canadian friend, to come back to the restaurant, she continued line-editing the blackboard. Tonkatsu, not Tonketsu. Okonomiyaki, not Okonomayaki. She was tired of what this German city of Nuremberg offered regarding Japanese food.

Maya looked out the huge windows. The restaurant was near the bus depot; she saw long-distance buses coming in and out. It was nearly 7 p.m. on a warm and sunny October day. The afterglow of the setting sun shone through the panes into the restaurant and painted the white tables amber. Allison showed up. She hugged Maya, threw her jacket and purse onto a stool, and sat down on another.

"Tell me everything," Allison said. "You said you've just visited your best friend from grad school in Tacoma, correct?"

"Yes," Maya said.

"And? You guys got … physical?"

Maya nodded. So much for their 8-year friendship, emailing, texting, Facetiming almost on a daily basis. She had been telling everyone that she had a twin soul brother. So, a friendship between a man and a woman didn't work, after all, you might say. But so what? She was feeling great.

Allison cheered up, raised her Muscadet glass and clinked it to Maya's. "YES!" she said and looked at Maya enviously. Allison was 45, married and had a long-term lover too, and still wanted to explore. Her husband didn't believe that women over 40 needed physical intimacy. Maya wasn't surprised; she had another friend like that, also in her 40s.

Maya was 48, divorced, and stayed in Germany to raise her children. Once she'd thought about going back to Japan, but her friends there had convinced her not to. *Don't come back. Your half-Japanese children would be bullied here, so would you. The only place you could live in would be Minato-ku Ward in Tokyo, where there is a sort of community for international people.* Maya found this funny because Minato-ku was one of the fanciest districts where country girls dreamt they might one day live, and would-be Minato-ku Girls were busy hunting sugar daddies to sustain their magazine-living ways. But surprisingly, Minato-ku had great supporting programs for single parents, or so she heard. Did Maya, a real Tokyoite, want to get back to her hometown to live inside the Minato-ku bubble? She wasn't sure.

The lighting in the restaurant dimmed. Their waiter asked them, in English, if everything was fine. Allison complained, in German, that they hadn't got their appetizer platter yet. She hated to be spoken to in English.

Soon they got their appetizer. "So, what are you guys going to do about the long-distance?" Allison asked.

"I don't know. We'll see. I'm used to long-distance."

"But you gotta live, Maya! You need to have *it* more! It's been like, a year since you last had sex before this one? You need balance!"

Maya knew. She was not much different from Allison, or from her other friend, for wanting more intimacy. The number 50 was flickering in front of her eyes. Perhaps it was not the fact that she would be turning that age soon, but rather the menopausal changes that she'd have to go through that frightened her.

All her life Maya had hated menstruation and ovulation. Both were painful. Ovulation not as much, but when mild pelvic pain stung her lower belly, she knew her egg for the month had sprung.

But that changed around the time she turned 40. Pains had become milder; instead, she began to suffer from an irresistible carnal desire crawling under her skin. And she knew she was ovulating.

Was it her biological clock that was torturing her? *Your time will soon be up, conceive now!* Why had sex, which was never that great in her 20s and 30s, suddenly begun to feel heavenly good in her 40s? What would happen when she turned 50 and beyond? Would she dry up? Would no man be interested in her anymore? Now, every month when she found a red stain on her panty, she couldn't help but be grateful for it.

And why the hell, she thought, was she wasting her time allowing herself to be down and alone for so goddamn long? She could count how many times she'd had sex in her 40s. She wished she could have been the type of person who could enjoy casual sex. She dared to try twice. One happened a year earlier in 2018, her sex-for-the-year, with someone she knew through her freelance work, so it was not a very clever move, but she took the chance. He was a few years older and couldn't perform. He then wanted to film them naked. He said he loved her and wanted to marry her. *Says the married man*, she thought. The other one had been a few years further back. It was okay. But the man started blackmailing her when she declined the invitation to do it a second time.

So, she'd quit. But she never felt like judging female friends who just wanted to have more experiences.

Maya and Allison ordered a second bottle of Muscadet. Allison didn't seem to be interested in Maya's best friend anymore, but instead, wanted to know Maya's opinion about her algebraic notion of penis sizes: height-weight relativity plus/minus/times racial stereotypes. Allison nibbled some edamame beans and licked the salt left on her thumb. She said she was happy to catch up with Maya because she couldn't talk about these things with her German friends. She went into details of her recent adventure, tantalizingly. She was wearing a pumpkin-coloured cashmere sweater and a pearl necklace. She looked like a *Madame*. No one around them would have imagined she was saying what she was saying.

"And you? Are you even trying to get social?" Allison asked, finishing off her glass.

"No."

"You should," Allison said. "Have you tried out those local matching get-together parties?"

"No," said Maya. Most people at such parties were Europeans. They told her how they loved Japan, or sushi, or asked at what age people retired in Japan, or how it felt to be a national of a country that had the Fukushima nuclear disaster. North Americans asked her what she did, what she liked to do, or what good films she'd seen recently. She liked that way better. "I'm not really looking for a relationship here."

"Okay, fair enough. But you gotta do *it* more! What about that app thing, that—"

"Tinder?"

"Yes, Tinder!" Allison snapped her fingers.

By the time they finished the third bottle, a lot of what they'd talked about had already slipped Maya's mind. She vaguely remembered that Vic, Allison's lover, picked them up at the restaurant. Maya woke up at home on the couch with her contact lenses still in her eyes. She went to the bathroom and saw herself in the mirror. Her favorite earrings were missing. "You look like shit," she said to herself.

She looked at her phone to check the time: 05:49. She tapped on the World Clock icon and wondered if she could write anything to her friend in Tacoma to cover the nine-hour time gap. Then she found the Tinder app downloaded on her phone. She had no idea why it was there. Allison, she thought, and deleted it.

It was still dark, but the edges of the neighbouring houses were yellowing. She went out on the balcony with a cigarette.

That had been a typical night out with Allison, and that was all right with Maya. Allison was a good-natured woman, just curious about what she would and would not miss out on for the rest of her life, just like many others in their 40s, or in their teenage years. Maya agreed with her: life goes on, and she's got to live. But what Maya missed was not only physical intimacy; Allison perhaps didn't understand.

Maya missed his tiny bachelor apartment on top of the hill in Tacoma. With no heat or external lighting at the end of September, she didn't have to feel the cold, for she had the warmth of having someone who shared the cold. She missed them making coffee for each other, slicing fruits for each other, apples for her and cantaloupes for him. She missed having breakfast on his balcony, with the slightly putrid "Tacoma Aroma" and the view of rodents gnawing garbage scattered on the ground that hadn't been recently collected, looking at the snowy silhouette of Mount Rainier against the orange sky, looming in between thin cedar trees. He, 46, was also working on wages, like herself, despite a master's degree, doing early shifts, managing a near-zero balance on his paid-time-off bank. No, a long-distance wouldn't work for the weary. It only worked for people with extra time and money. But she wasn't feeling all that blue because she had found her home. He was her home.

Maya went into the kitchen. She opened a package of coffee he'd given her, a blend named after a Scandinavian Goddess, roasted at a café in Tacoma. She put two spoonfuls of it into a paper filter, poured hot water into it and let it stand. The coffee smell soon drifted into the cold room.

That was her Tacoma Aroma.

A Blue Fish

A friend died. His small, grey Toyota crashed into a six-ton dump truck, right between the tires, as he tried to overtake a car in the wrong lane. A can of ginger ale lay crushed behind the brake pedal. Perhaps he'd left the empty can rolling about in the car and it was stuck behind the pedal, or perhaps the brake didn't work when he needed it, so said the police. He was on his way home from work as an intern at a junior high school. He knew his girlfriend was waiting in his room.

Like a crushed can of ginger ale was his body. Makeup couldn't mend the damaged corpse. A white cloth covered the small window of his plain wooden coffin, and we couldn't see his face for the farewell. All we could do was place a pile of white chrysanthemums on the coffin.

Right about then we heard a thud. Rei, his girlfriend, my close friend, collapsed on the floor. Immediately the black-clothed people formed a mountain over her. I pictured her under the tens of faces, curling up, sobbing, moaning, whining, yet I couldn't go to talk to her. What would I say? Are you OK? I'll be with you? Everything's going to be fine. Whatever I would say would sound fake. It wasn't me who'd lost my love. Speechless, I left the funeral.

"Thank you for the letter," Rei said to me a few weeks later. I'd written that I'd regretted I hadn't said anything to her at the funeral, and that I would be always there for her.

"You don't know how much I appreciated it. People who I didn't even know came up to me and said *I know*. I mean, it was nice of them, but"—Rei closed her eyes—"I just wanted to be left alone."

"I know," I said. She opened her eyes and looked at me. We laughed.

"Now, I'd like to ask a favour of you," she said.

"Which is?"

"I'd like to go to his Forty-ninth Day ceremony in his hometown. Can you keep me company?"

The Forty-ninth Day: a Buddhist ceremony for the dead to leave for *the other world*. Going to his hometown in Kagoshima prefecture meant going to the southernmost prefecture of the southernmost island of Japan's four main islands.

He, she, and I had all lived in Tsukuba City, which was about 60 kilometers northeast of Tokyo. We were students at the University of Tsukuba. The city was built for the university and some scientific institutions. An artificial landscape—boulevards crossed like a grid, uniformly tall trees flanked the streets. Cheap diners, apartments.

Here, everyone was an outsider. We'd all come from different parts of Japan, or the world. The strong dialect of the region didn't exist in this city. We had our own language, our own culture. In this heterogeneous space we had created a strange, para-familial commune.

A university girlfriend, however, wouldn't have the same legitimate influence as a wife would. His corpse was brought back to his home and for Rei, *c'est fini*. I sensed her hesitation to visit his family during this delicate time. I did quick mental arithmetic to see if I could afford flight tickets from the month's savings.

"Sure," I said after a while.

September in Japan is typhoon season. Flights were cancelled and cancelled, and we missed the Forty-ninth Day. Finally we had a chance to fly, though at the check-in counter we were informed about a possible rerouting due to an approaching typhoon to the Kyusyu area.

"What do you think?" Rei asked.

"Why not take a chance? We are here anyway."

We landed, as previously announced, at Miyazaki Airport in the neighbouring prefecture, instead of Kagoshima Airport. We decided to rent a car. As we lined up in front of a rental car service counter, a gigantic man behind us asked, "Where are you two going?"

We turned around. "To Kanoya City in Kagoshima," Rei said.

"I'm going in the same direction. Why don't you let me rent one and give you a ride?"

Rei and I looked at each other. Her eyes implied yes. How could students decline such an offer?

"Sure, that'll be great," I said.

The driver's seat of a white Suzuki *kei* car seemed too cramped for the man. I sat in the front seat, so I was the one who was expected to be social. "Were you on our flight?" I asked him.

"Yes." He turned his face toward me.

"Where are you going?"

"To Fukuoka."

"Fuku—Fukuoka?" I stuttered. "That's like a half-day drive from here!"

"My flight to Fukuoka was cancelled and ours was the only one available today. I have to go back to work tomorrow."

"What do you do?"

"I'm a prison guard on death row."

Thousands of questions came up in my mind. "What is it like?" I managed to ask.

The man didn't turn his face toward me. "Well ... I sometimes get boxes of chocolates from their families."

Silence fell. I gazed off into the view spread out in front of us. Trees had blown down, bowing over the highway from either side.

"I hear it was really stormy around this area yesterday. Some were even killed," he said.

I tried to recall the map of the area though I only had a dim memory of our geographic whereabouts. Going in the same direction, he had said, but if he was going to Fukuoka, it was probably a detour.

The tunnel of the fallen trees swallowed us. The Suzuki drove on, carrying our silence.

Two hours later we reached Kanoya City. The man asked directions only once, and with a grass-green sticky note in hand, he soon found the house of our deceased comrade. He wouldn't accept our offer to split the cost of the car and drove off.

It was an old, traditional Japanese wooden house. The teak walls had turned silvery grey over the years, yet the black tiles of the gabled roofs remained lustrous. No sooner had the car left than the front door of the house opened. A greying, middle-aged couple appeared. The woman craned her neck in the direction of the departed car and said, "Oh, has the taxi already left? We wanted to pay the fare ..."

"Oh, no. It wasn't a taxi." We explained what had happened.

His mother was short and chubby, his father tall and skinny. The pair looked just like those old couples in images from Japanese folk tales. A traditional husband and wife who called each other "*Otosan*, the father," and "*Okasan*, the mother." They never forgot to put smiles on their faces.

The father led us to the living room while the mother made green tea for us. We sat down on the tatami floor. Perhaps the tatami mats had just been replaced; I noticed their fresh, mint-like smell.

"We feel so bad for not picking you up at the airport," the father brought up again.

"We didn't know where we would land," Rei said. "Really, please don't feel bad. We were fine."

While they made small talk, I looked at photos of the family on the shelves. A young mother and a boy. Three boys and a dog. He was the middle child of three brothers, that I knew, so I figured that the boy of average height was he. I saw a familiar expression in the boy's face. In another picture a boy was playing soccer. Both he and his elder brother were soccer players at our university. Our university was famous for its team; we had some national league players.

The mother came into the living room with a tea set on a tray and noticed that I was looking at the pictures.

"Do you have any siblings?" she asked me.

"No. I'm an only child."

"Oh, then ...," *you must have been spoiled*, was what I thought would follow, because I'd heard that millions of times. An only child usually doesn't wear old clothes or have old toys, but this doesn't say anything about being spoiled. People judge people by what they have, not by what they don't have. "You must have been so lonely."

I raised my brows. "Yes."

"I was still not satisfied when I had two kids. Two was too few. We wanted to have one more," she said, and half smiled.

The father told us that their youngest son was also going to Tsukuba the following year. "They all have to travel so far just to play soccer," he said, and half smiled.

"I think the bath is ready," the mother said. "You must be tired after the long trip. Please relax until dinner is ready."

Japanese family members share the same water in the bathtub and guests usually take *Ichiban-buro,* the first bath. Rei was too tired to take a bath, so I was the first to go.

Immersed up to my chin in the hot water, I thought of the pictures I'd seen. Although he was my friend, I didn't have a strong bond to him like his parents and Rei did. I felt as if I'd been peeping into someone's history while that very person was absent. As if I'd been an actor on stage without any role. I wiggled in the bathtub awkwardly.

"We'll take you to a *Satsuma-age* restaurant tomorrow," the mother said in front of our guest bedroom. *Satsuma-age*, a deep-fried fish cake. Nothing fancy; there are many such mass-produced items in the chilled section of supermarkets. But I got a craving when she said that, in this restaurant, the cook fries them in the open kitchen in front of the guests. I suddenly recalled that *Satsuma* was the medieval name of Kagoshima. I went to bed dreaming of golden-brown crispy skins and the spongy white fish meat of a freshly fried *Satsuma-age*.

The restaurant was, however, closed the next day. His parents decided to take us to the coast instead. While we were waiting at the bus stop, I saw an old shed right in the middle of the yellowing rice fields. On the wall that faced us hung a huge billboard. Jodie Foster was smiling at us with a bottle of coffee beverage in her hand. An advertisement from years before. It had been in the sun and rain and lost its colour. It almost looked like a black and white picture.

The bus went uphill then downhill. From the windows, far below through the darkness of pine tree woods, I saw the ocean shine. The bus threaded through the woods and reached a beach.

It was a sunny day, but the water was grey. It wasn't like the white sand beaches on Phuket Island or the black sand beaches on the Canary Islands that I'd seen in magazines. It was a typical Japanese grey beach.

We strolled to the rockiest part, which was exposed during the ebb tide.

"Where are you from?" the mother asked me.

"Tokyo."

"Oh, then, life here must seem so different to you."

Before I had time to answer, Rei called me. "Hey, come over here, look!"

The mother and I went up to her. She crouched down, her knees bent to her chest, looking into a pool between the rocks.

There poised an inch-long, neon blue tropical fish.

"A tropical fish? I thought we only had them in Okinawa!" I said, because Kagoshima still belonged to the temperate zone. When I lowered my head toward the water in mild excitement, I heard the mother shout. "Otosan! Where are you going?"

Rei and I looked up. The father was a metre away from the shore, standing on a rock, his hands at his back, one wrist holding the other. Looking down at his feet, his shoulder stooped. And then he jumped onto the next rock, and onto the next.

"Otosan, don't go so far! It's dangerous!" the mother cried, yet the father didn't turn around. He kept leaping, like a little boy hopping on one foot and going farther and farther from the shore.

"Otosan, Otosaaan," she kept calling. The father didn't turn around. "*Come baaack!*" Her cry echoed in the air. I looked at her. Her cheeks were streaked with tears. I looked at him. He was still jumping over the rocks, hands clasped behind his back, his head drooped, his shoulders stooped.

Kai's Shoes

When we came to Canada in 2008, our children were 4 and 2. They didn't know a single English word.

A lot of people told us that the kids would get the language quickly; that the kids would be fine, they would come through. So, we threw our children into daycare.

My younger son was outgoing, but my elder son, Kai, was an introvert. He seldom joined circles or show-and-share. He played on his own.

Still, he was good at languages. He started to pick up some words. He stayed in daycare for four months, and then moved on to senior kindergarten at a public school in Oakville, Ontario.

At recess each day, Kai had no friends to play with.

"So, I walk," he said. "I walk and walk and walk for 10 long minutes."

On the schoolyard among basketball players and Beyblade fighters, I watched him walking. Walk, walk, walk, staring down at his toes.

How silly, how thoughtless I had been to believe the myth that he would instantly adjust. Kids were *not* all right just being thrown into such an unfamiliar milieu. Recently, I have learned from bilingually raised adults that being in settings where you don't understand a word is torture.

On Jan. 3, 2010, Kai was set to start Grade 1 the following day. I, meanwhile, was starting an internship at a prestigious publishing house in Toronto.

Kai was grumpy the whole day. In the evening, he started to weep, and said: "I don't want to go to school tomorrow."

I knew what he was feeling. I was 38 and experiencing similar anxiety.

I heaved him up into my arms and went to a quieter, darker room, away from my other son and my husband.

We sat on a sectional sofa, Kai on my lap. He stared at my face. His cheeks were still wet.

"Are you afraid of school because you have to speak English again?" I asked.

He blinked. "Yes."

"You know, I'm afraid of going to work tomorrow too. They may not understand my English."

My eyes welled.

"You, afraid?" His face lit up, half in amazement, half in doubt. I know how heroic parents can seem to young children. "Afraid" and "parents" don't match.

"Yes, I'm afraid," I said. "But I'll do my best. Would you also go to school tomorrow and do your best?"

He thought for a while, then nodded.

The next day, my colleagues were all friendly and the office cozy, but I was still nervous. I almost choked when I picked up the first phone call. Kai's hanging in there too, I told myself. I can do this.

Day by day, I became more relaxed. Kai never complained.

Three months later, I was at the playground beside the school one day. The playground was right beside the schoolyard and parking lot, and most kids and moms would dawdle there after school.

I felt sullen. I never liked being there. The playground politics seemed too much for me.

I didn't feel like being social in my second language, and as usual I was on the lawn, reading while I waited for Kai to finish playing.

When I looked up from my book, Kai wasn't there. I looked around. He was nowhere to be seen. I hopped up.

Seeing me searching around, a mom I didn't know said, "Kai went that way," pointing at the school building.

I scuttled to the school. Another woman stopped me. "Are you looking for Kai?"

And so did another.

At last, I saw him, together with a woman, walking across the parking lot. The woman waved at me.

"You're Kai's mom, aren't you? I found him in the washroom."

Relieved, I chided my son. "You have to tell me when you go away!"

And then the three of us walked back to the playground.

I didn't know any of these women, but they all knew that I was Kai's mother, and they knew each other.

"Oh, you found him?" another woman yelled to us.

I was abashed. All this time, while I was being afraid and cowardly, slumping over my books and shutting these women out, they had built up such a caring circle.

The next day, I stuffed my Rosenthal basket with cookies and juice boxes and went to the playground. I got to know Cynthia, Linda, and Deepa. There was even another Japanese mom, Mayumi.

The picnics went on until summer break and began again in September. In the winter, we brought hot chocolate in a Thermos and waited patiently for our kids to be done sledding down the schoolyard slope.

My son is now in Grade 3.

He glides through the basketball court on in-line skates with James and Brennan.

He's not looking down at his shoes. I'm not looking down at my books.

The boys come to me, hand in hand, and press me for a play date. Kai corrects my English and we all laugh.

"Everyone in my class loves me," Kai says. "Everyone loves me."

The Tree of Hope

When the day's last bus for Shibuya departs with a dull vroom, a woman appears at the bus stop. She undusts the silvery-white bench and plunks herself down on it. The small, hard bench has an armrest in the centre so she can't lie down on it. But that's okay. Her upright posture will disguise her sleep the whole night. The covered bus stop will shelter her from dew.

At this time of the day, everything feels less foreign. She was born into the bustle of Tokyo and that was where she belonged, or so she thought until she lost everything. Then her hometown began showing unknown faces to her.

She runs her forefinger over the scribbles on the bench next to her, her name she scratched with the tip of a safety pin a few months ago. *Nozomi*—hope. This wasn't a bad week after all, she thinks; she's got three retail assistant gigs at grocery stores. She recalls the other staff woman who gave away food samples with her yesterday; she used to live in a park with her male savior, but the "blue-tent" commune had been chased away because some international sports shows were coming to town, she said.

Nozomi unfolds a frayed piece of newspaper and spreads the months-old sudoku over her lap. Right then, a bumblebee settles on her naked, wrinkled toe. A bumblebee, on a chilly November night in this concrete jungle? For a short while she let it totter along her digits, its velvety coat warm and delicate on her skin. But she bobs her toe in spite of herself. The insect flies away. Immediately she regrets it. When was the last time she was touched by some living thing at all?

Repenting, she slumps over her sudoku. Wisps of her half-white hair on both sides curtain her face from the outer world. She falls asleep. The short pencil she filched from a big box furniture store falls from her hand and makes a light clack on the pavement.

Across from the bus stop, from the second floor of a liquor store, a man is watching her. He loves the midnight hours; his nagging mother downstairs is asleep, and he feels most alive. Living off his parents, he doesn't have to work during the day. He is 39.

Through the windows, through binoculars, he observes the bus stop on the other side of the street. There she is again, that filthy little grandma! Vexed, he tugs the curtain shut. Ever since that jarring old woman started to show up a few months ago, he hasn't been able to enjoy his view. He loves his view, and it must stay as it should be. That's why he complained when his neighbor had set up a dish antenna. And now this woman! He likes to scrutinize the commercial ads—images of young girls barely wearing clothes—posted on the acrylic panels of the bus stop, but she's always sitting in front of them. He is especially angry tonight because the poster is of his favorite girl idol group. How could he drive off that woman? He frantically looks around the room. Perhaps he could offer her some money. He looms over his piggy bank and bangs his fist down on it.

I should forget about the bumblebee on such a cold, rainy night, Nozomi thinks. Her naked toes are ice. *When I get to do some more freebie giveaways at the same supermarket, I might be able to buy a new pair of shoes.* She has a good feeling about this place and is hoping for possible employment. She looks forward to the coming week.

Raindrops fall from the barreled roof of the bus stop shelter, drawing a glassy drapery before her eyes. She smells the wet asphalt from the road, and the petrichor from the open space behind the bus stop, at the same time. Through the beads of raindrops, she sees the fuzzy yellow circle hovering above the liquor store. Those lights are always on in that window; warm rays emanate from within even this late. She tries to picture the resident of the room. Perhaps it's a student studying hard, or a youngster playing a video game. She half smiles.

When she is about to take the sudoku sheet out of her threadbare cloth bag, she sees, through the beads of raindrops, a man approaching the bus stop. It's almost 2 a.m. She braces herself for it. He comes walking straight toward her.

And he stops. Thin and tall, he looks much younger than she. His wet, long hair is bundled into a low ponytail. She cannot see his eyes well through his foggy glasses. "Excuse me." She hears him say amidst the tapping of rainwater. She doesn't say anything. "I live around here. I see you here every night," the man says. "I thought—perhaps you need some help, if you don't mind me saying that." His wording is rather polite, but she senses a marginal snit in his tone. "So I—I have this." He gropes in his right pocket and takes something out. He opens his palm in front of her: ¥50,000.

She is flummoxed. It's almost like a monthly welfare benefit. "What is ..."

"I'm not just giving it to you," he speaks over her, his face impassive. "I want you to move away and don't want you to come back here."

She has no idea why her moving away from here would be worth ¥50,000 to him. The bills are alluring. With that money, she could be under roofs for a few days, have some warm meals—perhaps fresh salads and coffee too—and take hot baths. She might even buy a new pair of shoes.

But she doesn't want to wander about for a new place again.

Once she was a vagrant. In the concourse of several subway stations, she would sit on a piece of cardboard, denuded by disdainful gazes passersby stealthily threw at her. She went with men who were strangers a few times. Soon she found a fugitive refuge in a commune in a park. There she met a few other women, all of whom had male partners who protected them from other men in the commune, or from teenagers on the prowl for a prey. But even these partners could have been predators. They expected their women to cook and tidy up their *homes*, spewed their anger on them when they wanted; the very situation from which these women had run away.

And Nozomi found this bus stop. There is no one else but her, no dispute over the spot, no scrambling over the bento meals thrown away hours before the expiration at a nearby convenience store. A volunteer gives her a bimonthly haircut at a church. Hallelujah.

The fifty thousand yen is flickering in front of her eyes.

But she thinks: *I've been fine. I'll be fine. Fine alone.*

"Er—thank you for your kind offer. But well, no, I can't move away from here," she says, finally. Silence falls. Then she notices his eyes behind the thick glasses—now cleared—leering. He turns livid. The rain is now harder, banging the panels of the bus stop, like those soybeans the Japanese throw at the beginning of the spring.

He comes one step forward to her. In his other hand is a 1.5-liter plastic bottle stuffed with stones. He breathes in, calmly, and jabs his left arm high in the air, over her head. He swings the bottle straight down on her. She topples. He holds his arm in the air once again, and gives her skull a wallop.

"No, I didn't know my sister had been living on the street," Nozomi's brother says. "No, we didn't know that," her on-call co-workers and high-school mates say. "She was a strong woman. She didn't say anything," is their phrase when newspapers report the late-night atrocity. Her mysterious life has stirred society.

People keep coming to the bus stop, offering flowers. Pink, orange, red. The flower wall creeps up the acrylic panels, and the bus stop turns into an island of flowers floating on the gray road.

The man across the street is still grumpy. Having managed to get rid of the skint woman, he still cannot enjoy the girls in the ads because of the flowers. In a fret, he goes out to the bus stop every night when the last bus is gone. Night after night, he buries flowers in the open space behind the bus stop. But people keep coming. Mostly women; some young, some not. Men come too. It is already December, but they find all kinds of flowers from shops and leave them there: magenta roses, purple dahlias, yellow lilies.

I hate roses! I hate lilies! The man mumbles while walking across the street. When he smells the scent of jasmine, he picks up the bouquet and smashes it against the panel. White petals fall swaying like feathers. He picks up another bouquet, and another, and throws them madly. He heaves as many wreaths and pots as he can take in his arms, brings them over to the open space behind the bus stop, and shoves them onto the ground. He crouches down. As he is thwacking the soil with a shovel, a voice pops up from behind, above his head: "Good evening." He turns his head around. Two police officers are standing there. "We have some questions for you."

The man stands up slowly.

The spring has come. The bus stop is still flowery; bumblebees are hopping on pistils. We don't know what kind of seeds the angry man has buried, but a sapling is growing inches above the soil in the open space. A year has passed. In the second spring, it has already grown into a tall tree, a broadleaf tree. It throws its leafy limbs into the sky; its round leaves give the tree a soft, round shape. From a distance, it looks like a huge green fist emerging in the blue.

In the summer, the tree drops shades and dapples the ground. People gather, standing in the gray clouds on the grass, under the verdant branches towering over them, over the bus stop. In the ruthless mugginess of the Tokyo summer, people still seem to want to get together and talk. Sometimes they have to raise their voices, among the buzzes of cicadas, and that makes them thirsty.

Soon an older woman sets up a tea stand there. She comes every day to this tree behind the bus stop. It is less flowery in the summertime heat, but there are always some withered bouquets left near the bench. When the woman doesn't have any more iced green tea to sell, she pours the rest half full into a plastic cup and sits down on the bench under the bus stop shelter.

A younger woman is often here, waiting for a bus. Every time she has to wait she buys a cup of tea at the stand. The icy liquid quenches her throat. The water-brewed green tea tastes almost sweet.

One day, on her way to the university, the young woman buys a cup of tea as usual and waits at the bus stop. Soon the tea vendor woman comes too, with a half-full cup, and sits down on the bench. She looks sideways. There is a kanji character scratched on the surface next to her. She looks up at the younger woman standing nearby. Their eyes meet, and they smile at each other. The older woman asks her shyly, pointing at the kanji on the bench: "Could you please tell me how to read this?"

The younger woman slightly bends over the bench for a better look at it. She raises her brows lightly, and answers, "Nozomi." And then she says: "It's the name of a woman who used to spend nights at this bus stop and was killed by a man for no reason."

"Good name," the older woman says. "I remember watching the news on TV in a bath house. Brutal, brutal man. It must have been nice to live here though. It's a nice place." Her neck abruptly drops backwards as if she had dozed off on a train. She looks up at the tree. Birds warble among the leaves.

The younger woman observes the woman resting on the bench. Her dark-blue cotton blouse is tattered, her hair disheveled from sweat, smelling slightly putrid. "Do you live near here?" the younger woman asks.

"I live everywhere."

The young woman ponders for a while. "Do you have a place to go?"

The older woman shakes her head.

"Any family members? Friends?"

"I have a son, but he's married, you know."

"Have you tried those—social services?"

"You know," the older woman says, "I barely finished junior high school. I can't read. I can't write. Computers, forget it." She has an accent, but the younger woman cannot tell what it is.

"If you need help with filling out application forms for public assistance," the younger woman says hesitantly, "perhaps I could help you."

"Thank you, dear," the older woman says. "But—I don't think I want to change anything anymore. I'm already 70." She cracks a smile. Her cheekbones rise, deep lines fanning out around her eyes. "I used to live in one of those shelters. The staff was nice, social workers were nice … They were like parents; they controlled my allowance, or reminded me what time I should take pills, stuff like that." She chuckles. "But sometimes,"—she pauses on a word—"tame, yes, tame. Sometimes I felt they wanted to tame me. So I could become a standard Japanese woman. Good, *clean*, docile wife kind of person," she says, and laughs out loud. "Not many, but a few people even seemed to be thinking homelessness or prostitute-ness is something curable, like a disease."

The younger woman has listened. "I'm sorry," she says quietly.

"I'm no rebel," the 70-year-old says. "I wasn't declining their protection or anything like that. Who'd want to live on the street?" She drinks the last sip of her green tea. "But … sometimes I just wanted to decide on things myself. I just wanted to be myself."

The older woman stands up. She walks away from the bus stop, to her tea stand under the tree. At the curb, she turns around to the other woman. "It was nice chatting with you," she says. "It's so nice to talk with women. I've never shared with anyone that I can't really read."

The summer is over, but the tree still invites people. There are some adjustments to the bus routes and this bus stop becomes no longer in use. A group of volunteers makes efforts and keeps the bus stop shelter. They move the shelter with the bench, on which Nozomi's name is still carved, closer to the tree.

The evergreen tree grows and grows. Its fist spurts high in the sky. The tree invites women to talk. The sunshine comes through yellowing leaves, making them shine silver and lighting up the whole area. Leaves rustle in the wind; people attune to the language of the tree. "Open up," as if it were saying. "It's okay to talk—okay to ask for help," as if Nozomi were whispering.

Soon the city will build some social housing for women in need, run by women, next to the bus stop, people have heard. A branch of the Employment Service Center for women has opened; they strive to find better-paying full employment for their visitors so that they could receive benefits, not welfare—higher payment, less intervention in privacy—like many men. A group of women has started reading and writing lessons on the grass under the tree, with glasses of green tea. The university student, who talked to the tea vendor woman, is now one of the volunteers to teach the lessons. When the tea vendor woman is not selling tea or joining the lessons, she helps the soup kitchen near the tree. She serves soup not only for women; men in need frequent the kitchen too.

People still gather under the tree.

Nozomi no ki—the Tree of Hope, someone begins to call it.

Acknowledgements

First and foremost, I must thank Rob Jackson. A musician and writer himself, he used to be one of the publishers of *Great Lakes Review*. Ever since he published "A Perfect Day to Die" in his journal, he has championed my writing. Without his enthusiasm and unconditional support, this collection could not exist.

I often swapped stories for tandem reviews with the writers Tanaz Bhathena, Mayank Bhatt, and Jason Cooke. I miss those days.

Fraser Sutherland, who passed away in early 2021, was the first reader of many of my stories. I will feel the pain of his absence forever and miss his cutting remarks and encouragements every time I finish a story.

I somehow began feeling the urge to write fiction in the middle of the Post-secondary Journalism program at Sheridan College, Oakville, Ontario. There I met two wonderful writing mentors and powerful role models for women: Katherine Govier and Patricia Bradbury.

Thanks to all the literary journals that published my stories; you have no idea how I turned into a happy drunk dancer every time I received an acceptance letter.

To T, who found me and read my stories during the COVID lockdowns. I couldn't have survived the darkness without conversations with him and his music.

And to Michael Mirolla and the fantastic team at Guernica Editions.

About the stories: there is a song in Japan in the 80s called "Shorto Sunzen," meaning "at the verge of short circuit," by the Japanese rock band called Barbee Boys. It is about a weepy comedian who drinks, eats chocolate bars, throws his mascots onto the wall on Sundays. So, he is actually more like Nina than my comedian, but I was very inspired by how he expressed his loneliness.

As for the ants' ecology, I primarily referred to Dr. Hidehiro Hasegawa's book and papers, among others.

I'd like to dedicate "Gustafson and the Chinese" to Kitty, a Hongkong woman I used to know in Germany, who fought a losing battle against lung cancer and had to leave two young daughters behind to her unfaithful husband. I am sorry for my poor attempt to describe your city and your situation.

The stories were originally published in the following journals:

"A Perfect Day to Die" *Great Lakes Review* (USA), 2012.
"St. Clair West" *untethered* (Canada), 2016.
"The Comedian" *Flash Fiction Online* (USA), 2018.
"The Man Who Sells Clouds" *The Montreal Review* (Canada), 2012.
"The Summer with No Mosquitoes" *Great Lakes Review* (USA), 2018.
"What the Ant Said" *LooseLeaf* (Canada), 2018.
"Nobu's Writing Therapy" *The Red Line* (UK), 2015.
"Gustafson and the Chinese" *Great Lakes Review* (USA), 2013.
"April Fools' Day" *CommuterLit* (Canada), 2018.
"Soda Pop Candy" *Active Muse* (India), 2019.
"A Blue Fish" *Salon.II.* (Linda Leith Publishing, Canada), 2012.
"Kai's Shoes" Originally developed for *The Shoe Project* (Canada) as "Walking"; published as "A Canadian Welcome" in *The Globe and Mail* (Canada), 2012.
"The Tree of Hope" *Narratives on Women's Issues Volume 2: Women Power* by International Human Rights Art Festival in New York, December 2021.

About the Author

Originally from Tokyo, Yoko Morgenstern started writing fiction while living in Canada, inspired by many writers who wrote in a second language. Yoko is the author of *Double Exile* (Red Giant Books, Cleveland. 2014) and *Eigo no Zatsudanryoku* (Gento-sha, Tokyo. 2014), and a regular contributor to *Newsweek Japan*. This short story collection was a finalist for Eyelands Book Awards, in the unpublished short story collection category, in Greece in 2019. Some of the stories have been translated into Brazilian Portuguese. In 2021, she wrote "The Tree of Hope" for the anthology titled *Women Power* curated by the International Human Rights Art Festival, New York. She translates, too. Her Japanese translation of *The Ghost Brush* by the Canadian novelist Katherine Govier was long-listed for the Japan Translation Award in 2015. She received a B.A. in Political Science from the University of Tsukuba, Japan, a Post-graduate Diploma in Journalism from Sheridan College, Oakville, Ontario, and an M.A. in English and American Studies from the University of Bamberg, Germany. She is an official member of the Japan P.E.N. Club and Die Kogge (European Authors Association). Currently, she lives in Nuremberg, Germany.

Printed in April 2022
by Gauvin Press,
Gatineau, Québec